MATCH WITS WITH TRIXIE!

Trixie Belden has a thrilling challenge for you!

Match wits with Trixie as she solves some baffling mysteries and grapples with some perplexing quizzes.

Test your powers of observation with ingenious cartoon mysteries. Spot the hidden clue! It's in there, somewhere—but you have to be sharp to see it!

Minute mysteries challenge your deductive skills. Unravel the clues and find the villain. You have to be quick, though—or the villain might escape!

Dozens of quizzes on all sorts of subjects mystify your mind. There are even cryptic quizzes in code for you to decipher!

And here's an extra-special bonus—a Trixie Belden short story for you to enjoy!

So sharpen your pencils and your wits and join America's favorite girl detective for mystery, adventure—and fun!

Trixie Belden
MYSTERY-QUIZ BOOK Number 1

BY KATHRYN KENNY
with
Joan Bowden
Mary Carey
Eileen Daly
Laura French
D.J. Herda
and others

•

Illustrated by
Jack Wacker and Erv Gnat

Cover by Jim Wagner

•

®.GOLDEN PRESS
Western Publishing Company, Inc.
Racine, Wisconsin

CONTENTS

FINGERPRINTS

"Trixie," Honey said as she slipped into a chair beside her friend at the library, "I just found some interesting stuff about fingerprints."

Trixie paged through the book Honey had put in front of her. "Hm!" she said after a while. "I didn't know this about identical twins. . . ." She settled down to read further.

What do you know about fingerprints? Here's a quiz to help you find out. Answer **true** or **false**.

1. Fingerprint patterns are formed before birth.

2. Only on the fingertips can we find the ridge designs that make prints.

3. Although no two fingerprints are alike, they all follow a few basic patterns of whorls, loops, and arches.

4. Identical twins have identical fingerprints.

5. A print on the left forefinger is the same as the print on the right forefinger of an individual.

6. If an injury to a fingertip causes a scab to form and fall off, the print always grows back in the same pattern.

7. If one finger on a hand has a loop pattern, the other fingers all have loop patterns.

8. Some persons, unable to write, have "signed" wills and contracts with their fingerprints.

9. Ridge designs that make the prints have remained on fingers months after the person has died—and they have been used as clues.

10. A criminal who has had skin grafted to his fingertips to make them absolutely smooth need never worry again about being arrested on the basis of fingerprint evidence.

MYSTERY AT WIMPY'S

Trixie and her brothers Mart and Brian go to Wimpy's with Honey Wheeler and Jim Frayne. Both of the girls and one of the boys have hamburgers, and the other two boys have cheeseburgers. Two of the three who have hamburgers have chocolate shakes, and the other three have vanilla shakes. Jim has the same kind of burger that Trixie has, and his shake is the same flavor as Honey's. What does each of the five have to eat and drink?

HINT: A good way to solve this kind of quiz is to chart the clues.

Example:

hamburger	hamburger	hamburger	cheeseburger	cheeseburger
girl	*girl*	*boy*		

THE CASE OF THE TRICKY TATTOOS

Trixie is investigating a robbery in which there are four suspects: Donna the Dip, Dapper Dave, Jailbird Joe, and Carol the Con. Trixie has these clues:

1) Three of the suspects are right-handed, and three of them have tattoos on the opposite wrist from the hand they write with.

2) Neither Dapper Dave nor Jailbird Joe has a tattoo on his left wrist, but both Jailbird Joe and Carol the Con have scars under their left eyes.

3) Donna the Dip writes with a different hand than Dapper Dave does.

4) The guilty suspect has no tattoos on either wrist.

Which of the four committed the robbery?

THE CASE OF THE AMATEUR BURGLAR

"This burglar can't even burgle," Trixie said disgustedly when Honey showed her this picture in the **Sleepyside Sun.** "Look at all his mistakes! He must be really new at the job." See how many mistakes you can find.

THE GUEST

Trixie Belden had her arms filled with books when she rang the doorbell of the Manor House.

"Well, hi!" said Honey Wheeler, who opened the door. She took several big books from Trixie. "What's up? You look like a traveling library."

"I had to do a paper for European history, and Jim loaned these to me," Trixie said. "Is he home? I promised I'd return them when I finished."

Before Honey could answer, a slim, dark-haired man came down the stairs. He paused when Honey turned toward him.

"Trixie, this is our guest, Mr. Ivanescu," Honey said.

The man bowed.

"Mr. Ivanescu met our friends, the Bronsons, in Paris," Honey went on. "They asked him to call my parents."

"And I am most happy to oblige," said the man. He spoke with a strong accent. "Mrs. Wheeler was so kind as to ask me to stay here in this beautiful place. I travel much on business, and one gets tired of hotels."

"The Manor House *is* beautiful," Trixie agreed. "Is your home in Paris?"

"It is now, but it was not always so," Mr. Ivanescu told her. "I was born in Romania, in a village in the Carpathian Mountains."

"The Carpathians?" Trixie brightened up. "Isn't Dracula's castle in the Carpathians?"

"Dracula?" For an instant, the guest looked puzzled. Then he laughed. "Ah, yes. The vampire count that some so-clever person made up. I know of him. Sometimes in Europe, they still show the motion picture in the theaters. But if you will excuse me, please? I am keeping Mr. and Mrs. Wheeler waiting."

Mr. Ivanescu bowed again and went into the drawing room. A moment later, Trixie and Honey heard him conversing with Honey's parents.

"Honey," Trixie said in low, urgent tones, "I think your mother should telephone the Bronsons right away and ask how well they know that man. I think he's a fake!"

Why did Trixie suspect the Wheelers' guest?

MUSEUM
MYSTERY

1. WHAT A PERFECT IDEA TO COME TO SEE THE NEW EXHIBITS TODAY.

LOOK AT THAT WHALE! HOW COULD THEY CATCH SOMETHING THAT BIG WITH THOSE LITTLE HARPOONS?

NORTH POLE

2. SOMETHING'S WRONG HERE, BUT I CAN'T FIGURE OUT WHAT IT IS. LET'S COME BACK WHEN THEY FINISH WORKING.

3. I'D SURE LIKE TO SEE THE REAL PYRAMIDS THESE MUMMIES CAME FROM.

ME, TOO... AND RIDE DOWN THE NILE ON ONE OF THESE BARGES, LIKE CLEOPATRA DID.

ANCIENT EGYPT

4 I'D RATHER RIDE IN THAT PIRATE SHIP.

LOOK AT ALL THE TREASURE! I THOUGHT PIRATES ONLY TOOK GOLD AND JEWELS.

PIRATE TROVES

5 I'M SORRY, BUT WE'LL HAVE TO ASK YOU TO GO THROUGH OUR METAL DETECTOR BEFORE YOU CAN LEAVE. A PRICELESS GOLD STATUE CALLED "THE LAUGHING BUDDHA" IS MISSING FROM ITS PLACE IN OUR HISTORY OF INDIA EXHIBIT.

6 YOU DON'T HAVE IT. YOU'RE FREE TO GO. I CAN'T UNDER-STAND IT, THOUGH. YOU'RE THE ONLY ONES WHO HAVE ENTERED THE MUSEUM SO FAR TODAY.

EXIT

7 NO, WE'RE NOT. THERE ARE WORKMEN AND GUARDS HERE, TOO. ONE OF THE WORKMEN IS THE THIEF. HE MADE A BIG MISTAKE WHEN HE HID THE STATUE. YOU MAY EVEN FIND HIS FINGERPRINTS STILL ON IT. I'M SURE IT'S IN...

EXIT

WHERE DID TRIXIE TELL THE OFFICIAL TO LOOK FOR THE STATUE?

A QUETZAL IN A WILLIWAW?

"Did you ever see a quetzal with a grivet in a williwaw?" Mart asked, obviously savoring the sound of the words.

"Never! And I don't think you did, either!" Trixie retorted.

"No," Mart admitted. "But it sounds interesting. Let's see how many of these things we can identify."

1. Santa Ana, harmattan, and williwaw are all
   a. trains.   b. winds.   c. places to live.

2. Gneiss, shale, and basalt are all
   a. rocks.   b. head coverings.   c. fertilizers.

3. Grivet, bandicoot, and peccary are all
   a. bad characters.   b. tools.   c. animals.

4. Bogotá, Osaka, and Kiev are all
   a. games.   b. cities.   c. streets.

5. Papaw, sweetsop, and pomelo are all
   a. fruits.   b. games.   c. words of endearment.

6. Collard, okra, and leek are all
   a. coins.   b. vegetables.   c. chemicals.

7. Borzoi, Basenji, and Samoyed are all
   a. Oriental ballets.   b. dialects.   c. dogs.

8. Hydrofoil, dugout, and junk are all
   a. vessels.   b. baseball equipment.   c. places for trash.

9. Canon, fugue, and sonata are all
   a. military weapons.   b. clothing.   c. musical compositions.

10. Shrike, bittern, and quetzal are all
    a. birds.   b. weather terms.   c. cloth measures.

SPORTS VARIETY

Basketball is probably the favorite sport of most of the Bob-Whites, but they know a lot about other sports, too. Dan Mangan scored 100 on this quiz in forty seconds flat. How long will it take you? Just match the sport on the left with the appropriate terms on the right. Ready, set, go!

1. basketball   a. shell, stroke, coxswain
2. hockey   b. net, drive, shuttlecock
3. tennis   c. crossbar, plant, takeoff
4. rowing   d. free kick, crossbar, volley
5. bowling   e. foul, umpire, mound
6. football   f. net, center forward, spike
7. bobsledding   g. sinker, reel, net
8. soccer   h. alley, net, love
9. golf   i. alley, frame, turkey
10. badminton   j. driver, stroke, bogey
11. fishing   k. foul, net, slam dunk
12. baseball   l. bowler, umpire, bails
13. cricket   m. heat, ballast, bob
14. pole vault   n. free kick, shoulder pads, crossbar
15. volleyball   o. slap shot, net, puck

QUICKIE QUIZ #1

Thanks to reading stories to their younger siblings, Trixie, Mart, Brian, and Di can name all seven of the dwarves who befriended Snow White. Can you? And can you tell the name of the handsome prince in the story?

A DRINK
OF COOL
WATER

"Trixie!" Mrs. Belden called up the stairs. "I know you're looking forward to the Memorial Day picnic, but would you run an errand for me before you leave, please?"

"Sure, Moms." Trixie started downstairs.

"I promised Ethel Elliot that I'd send over a loaf of banana bread if I baked today," said Mrs. Belden. "Would you wrap one of the loaves that are cooling in the kitchen and take it to her?"

A few minutes later, Trixie was on her bike and pedaling down Glen Road.

When she reached the little house, which stood at the end of a lane off Glen Road, Mrs. Elliot was on the porch, smiling at her.

The old lady's smile grew even wider at the sight of the wrapped loaf of bread in Trixie's hands. "Come in!" she said. "Your mother didn't forget, did she? How very nice of her."

"Moms is pretty good about not forgetting things," said Trixie. She followed Mrs. Elliot into the house and to the kitchen, where she put the loaf down on the table.

"You're a dear to ride over on such a warm day," Mrs. Elliot said. "Would you like a drink of nice, cool water?"

"Thanks," Trixie said. "I *am* thirsty."

But before Mrs. Elliot could get a glass from the cupboard, the doorbell rang. The old lady left Trixie in the kitchen and went to the front of the house. She returned in a few moments. "It's just the mail carrier," she said. "He's thirsty, too. He asked if he could have a drink of water."

"Did you get a special delivery order for some of your beautiful flowers?" Trixie asked.

"No, dear," Mrs. Elliot said. "It's just the regular mail."

Trixie looked startled. "Did you let him in?"

"Why, of course, dear," said the old lady.

Trixie went to the kitchen telephone and began to dial. "I'm calling the police," Trixie said in a low voice. "I don't know who you let in just now, but it isn't the mail carrier!"

Why was Trixie alarmed?

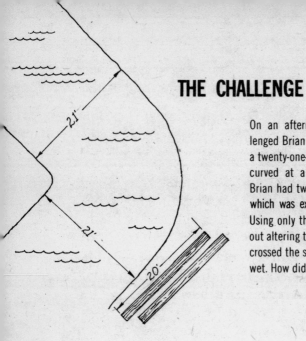

21'

21'

20'

THE CHALLENGE

On an afternoon hike, Jim challenged Brian to find a way to cross a twenty-one-foot-wide stream that curved at a ninety-degree angle. Brian had two logs to use, each of which was exactly twenty feet long. Using only the two logs, and without altering them in any way, Brian crossed the stream without getting wet. How did he do it?

R U 4 K9's, 2?

Can you translate this conversation? (Watch out for Mart's fancy words!)

Mart: R u bz?

Trixie: Y, s. Y?

Mart: I m nez.

Trixie: Y r u nez?

Mart: I c a cd k9.

Trixie: U kn c a tp n a (10)mn!

Mart: I 1dr f nel l's c's m.

Trixie: I c m, 2. E sn cd—e's a qt!

Mart: O, u r n li f l k9's. S bavr s dv8.

Trixie: Nel kn c e's b9.

Mart: Ok, ok. I kn c e's a b9 k9, 2. Xq's ME!

SPELUNKING

"What's SPEE-lunking, Mart?" little Bobby Belden asked.

"Cave exploring." Mart showed Bobby a picture in a book. "Spelunkers have to carry lights. They have to mark their trails, too, so they can find their way **out** of the caves."

"I want to go cave 'sploring," Bobby said.

"Me, too," Mart told him. "But first, let's look at this book some more."

In Mart's book were the answers to these quiz questions:

TRUE FALSE

1. Most of the estimated thirty thousand caves in North America have been explored.

       — —

2. "Cave pearls" are formed in a way similar to sea pearls.

       — —

3. Cave creatures—fish, insects, salamanders—that live in total darkness are not only blind but often eyeless.

       — —

4. Some stalactites grow an inch a year; others need a hundred years to grow an inch.

       — —

5. How did a cow help make a discovery?

It is said that a cow named Millicent revealed the entrance to what is now the Howe Caverns in New York.

On hot, sunny afternoons, Millicent would stand in a certain spot in a rocky pasture. This led observant spectators to their important discovery.

What was Millicent enjoying that led to the discovery of the caverns?

THE SLEEPING PILOT

Panel 1: THANKS FOR HELPING ME CARRY THESE CLOTHES TO ELLA, TRIXIE. SHE'LL GET THEM ALTERED IN TIME FOR THE BAZAAR.

SHE'S SUCH A POPULAR SEAMSTRESS THAT WE'RE LUCKY SHE HAS TIME TO DO THEM.

Glen Road Inn

Panel 2: THERE ARE POLICE ALL OVER THE INN. THE RUMORS ARE THAT THERE'S A DRUG SMUGGLER HERE.

HOW AWFUL!

Panel 3: HE WAS JUST TWO DOORS FROM ELLA!

Panel 4: I DIDN'T DO ANYTHING WRONG! I WAS SO TIRED THAT I WENT TO BED AT NINE O'CLOCK LAST NIGHT AND DIDN'T WAKE UP TILL MY ALARM WENT OFF THIS MORNING.

YES. HE'S A PILOT, AND SOMETIMES HE STAYS HERE BETWEEN FLIGHTS. HE USUALLY RETIRES VERY EARLY AND GETS UP LATE. THE RESPONSIBILITY FOR FLYING ALL THOSE PEOPLE MUST BE QUITE A STRAIN.

⑤

THERE'S HIS ROOM, HONEY. LET'S JUST LOOK...

⑥

SEE...HE WAS TELLING THE TRUTH. HE MUST HAVE TOSSED AND TURNED ALL NIGHT.

⑦

NO, HE TOLD ONE LIE THAT MAKES ME THINK THAT HE PROBABLY IS THE SMUGGLER.

⑧

WHAT LIE HAD TRIXIE CAUGHT THE PILOT IN?

SNEAK THIEF

Brian Belden pulled his jalopy to the curb in front of Mr. Van Stratten's gate. "You sure you want to do this?" he said to Trixie. "I wouldn't, if I were you."

"Scared of a couple of geese?" Trixie teased.

"Just respectful," Brian declared.

"I can outrun them any day," declared Trixie as she slipped out of the car. "Mr. Van Stratten," she yelled as she released the catch on the gate, "open the door!"

Trixie dashed up the walk to the house. The gate slammed shut behind her, and a pair of geese came flapping and hissing from a pond in the corner of the yard and tried to intercept her.

The front door of the house swung open in the nick of time, and Trixie slipped in and slammed it shut behind her. The geese hissed angrily on the porch.

"Those birds sure can move!" said Trixie.

"Not as fast as you can," chuckled Mr. Van

Stratten. "Well now, what was it you wanted to see me about?"

"We're having a raffle," Trixie told him. She took a ball-point pen and a book of raffle tickets out of the pocket of her Windbreaker. "It's to raise money for uniforms for the school baseball team. I know you always go to the ball games and . . ."

"I'd love to take a ticket," said Mr. Van Stratten. "In fact, I'll take a whole book of tickets. But not this morning. You see, we had a sneak thief during the night. He must have broken the glass in the library window, then opened the latch and got in. He took all the cash out of my wallet and everything from Mrs. Harrison's handbag."

"Mrs. Harrison?" echoed Trixie.

"My new housekeeper," said Mr. Van Stratten as he showed Trixie the broken window. Jagged pieces of glass lay on the porch outside. "I'll sweep that up after the police come," said Mr. Van Stratten. "They always say you should never touch anything. Not that it will do any good. I have a feeling the thief is over in the next county by now."

"I don't," said Trixie abruptly. "I have two reasons to believe that the thief is right here in this house!"

What were Trixie's reasons?

ABOUT THIS AND THAT

"Is a gallon always a gallon?" Diana wanted to know. "Here's a quiz that asks about that and a lot of other interesting things."

Answer **true** or **false.**

1. A gallon of milk weighs less than a gallon of gas.

2. Most folks eat only ninety percent of an egg.

3. The name of the man who discovered Angel Falls is Lucifer.

4. The highest mountain in the world could disappear from sight if it were dropped into the ocean.

5. The Hawaiian alphabet has twice as many letters as our alphabet.

6. If you have running water in a sink, you can tell if you are in the northern or southern hemisphere.

7. Easter never falls on March 21.

8. The plural of *man-of-war* is *men-of-war*, but the plural of *ottoman* is *ottomans*.

9. It takes more than one banana to get enough banana oil to fill a bottle of fingernail polish.

10. An ostrich really can fly; most of them just choose not to.

MR. LYTELL'S GENERAL STORE

One person who often appears in Trixie's mysteries is Mr. Lytell,
the owner of a general store on Glen Road. Here is a picture of one
part of his store. Study it for just one minute, then turn the page
and answer the questions without peeking back.

MR. LYTELL'S GENERAL STORE (continued)

If the Bob-Whites purchased everything you saw in Mr. Lytell's store (page 27), could they use the items to

1. sweep the floor?
2. shave a mustache?
3. chop wood?
4. decorate a Christmas tree?
5. build a fire?
6. find a job?
7. make a sandwich?
8. drink hot chocolate?
9. keep their hands warm?
10. till the garden?
11. knit a sweater?
12. go jogging?
13. plant seedlings?
14. mail a letter?
15. lock a door?
16. dig a hole?
17. keep their heads warm?
18. attach two pieces of paper together?
19. fry an egg?
20. pound a nail?

BAFFLERS

Jim said, "Here's a quiz that might baffle even you, Trixie. I'll say I'm an object and give you three clues. If you don't recognize me from the first clue, use the second, then the third."

1. WHAT AM I?

Clue #1: "I am supposed to point to something most people say is not really there—but which many would like to have."

* * * * *

Clue #2: "Everything has to be just right or I won't appear, but when I do, I'm often admired."

* * * * *

Clue #3: "I am quite colorful. Billions of people have seen me, but no one has ever touched me."

2. WHAT AM I?

Clue #1: "I never move—I have just one leg—but you can't go far in the city without meeting me."

* * * * *

Clue #2: "I am quite silent, but if you approach me, you'd better do as I say. Otherwise, you might be in trouble of one kind or another."

* * * * *

Clue #3: "I can't see, but I have three eyes to guide you, and you usually follow my directions."

3. WHAT AM I?

Clue #1: "I am recognized almost everywhere and often welcomed for what I bring."

* * * * *

Clue #2: "I am not worth much until I age a lot. Sometimes folks value me only for my faults."

* * * * *

Clue #3: My face is distinguished, but I am very small, usually measuring only an inch or so."

SLEEPYSIDE BANK MYSTERY

Trixie's merry blue eyes were sparkling as she hurried into Sleepyside's First National Bank. This was a day she had been looking forward to. Her banker father was going to take her to lunch.

"Sit down, Trixie," Peter Belden called to her, smiling. "I'll be with you in a minute."

He turned back to the young woman seated by his desk. "I understand you wish to borrow some money from our bank, Ms. Clarendon?"

"Yes, I do," answered the dark-haired young woman. "I want the bank to lend me five hundred dollars. I'm willing to put this up as security for the loan."

Trixie couldn't resist peeking over the top of her magazine to see what "this" was. She looked just in time to see Ms. Clarendon give her father what appeared to be a large book.

"It's only one of my many albums," Ms. Clarendon explained, "but it contains some of my most valuable stamps. In New York City, I am a very well-known stamp collector. Surely you, too, have heard of the philologist Clarissa Clarendon."

"I'm afraid not," Mr. Belden answered. "But I don't pretend to be an expert in that field. If you would care to leave your album here, however, I'll arrange for one of our bank officials who is more knowledgeable about stamps to examine the album later—"

"But I need the money now, not later," Ms. Clarendon protested. "Look at these stamps! *I'm* trusting *you* with them, and they're worth thousands of dollars! Take my word for it!"

Trixie couldn't bear to listen for another second. She hurried to her father's side and whispered into his ear.

Peter Belden rose to his feet at once. "My daughter has just reminded me of something that I should have remembered myself," he said. "And because of it, Ms. Clarendon, I'm afraid I cannot take your word for anything."

What did Trixie tell her father?

FAMOUS FICTIONAL DETECTIVES

Mart often teases Trixie and Honey by calling them "schoolgirl shamuses," but he's really very proud of them and considers them as clever as any of these famous fictional detectives. Can you name them all?

1. Humphrey Bogart played this detective in the movie, **The Maltese Falcon.**

2. This detective had an assistant named Watson.

3. Agatha Christie created this old-lady sleuth.

4. When this comic-book character plays detective, he calls himself "The Spider."

5. The real occupation of this sleuth is a priest.

6. This popular television-show detective is played by James Garner.

7. A raincoat and a cigar are the trademarks of this television sleuth.

8. These brothers were amateur sleuths in a book series; later, they appeared in a television series.

9. This police detective does his sleuthing in the Pink Panther movies.

10. A girl detective in a book series sometimes appeared with the brothers in #8 in their television series.

11. The radio program that featured this invisible sleuth always started with this question: "Who knows what evil lurks in the hearts of men?"

12. This lovable Chinese-Hawaiian-American detective had eleven children and lived on Punchbowl Hill.

13. This lawyer-detective, famous in books long before he was featured in a television series, was created by Erle Stanley Gardner.

14. This amateur detective is only ten years old, but he solves crimes (anonymously) for his police-chief father.

15. What is the name by which television detectives Jill Munroe, Kelly Garrett, and Tiffany Welles are known collectively?

TONGUE TANGLERS

Sometimes, when she gets excited, Trixie's words run together. She has to really concentrate in order to say these tongue tanglers. See how many times you can say each one correctly in one minute.

1. lemon liniment
2. Some shun sunshine.
3. A noisy noise annoys an oyster.
4. a blue bucket of blue blueberries
5. I never felt felt that felt like that felt felt.
6. Six slim slick slender chicks sit sunning by the shore.

THE COM-PANION

5. TRIXIE, YOU'RE A DEAR TO DO THIS FOR ME. BOBBY, TOO. WAIT JUST A MINUTE TILL I PAY BELLA FOR THE FUEL OIL THAT CAME TODAY, THEN WE CAN GO IN THE LIVING ROOM AND VISIT FOR A WHILE. I THINK I HAVE SOME OF BOBBY'S FAVORITE COOKIES.

6. YOU'LL HAVE TO MAKE OUT THE CHECK, BELLA. THEN I'LL SIGN IT.

7. WOULD YOU BELIEVE THAT THE MAN WHO DELIVERS THE FUEL CAME SO EARLY THIS MORNING THAT I WASN'T EVEN AWAKE! BELLA HAD TO PAY HIM WITH HER OWN MONEY.

8. DON'T SIGN THIS CHECK, MRS. GARBER. THE OIL MAN WASN'T HERE TODAY, AND I CAN PROVE IT!

HOW COULD TRIXIE PROVE IT?

A FAMOUS PAINTING

The prim PTA president walked quickly toward them. "Ah, Trixie and Honey," Mrs. Osilius said, smiling. "Now that you're here, the meeting of the student art committee can begin at once."

She drew them into one of the side rooms where several boys and girls were already seated. In front of them was a large covered easel.

"As you know," Mrs. Osilius began, "our generous students voted last month to donate a painting to our school building. Ever since that time, I've been searching for exactly the right one. At last I've found it! If you, as their representatives, approve, it will hang proudly in the entrance hall."

The students gasped as Mrs. Osilius slowly uncovered a large painting. Entitled simply "Moving Day," it showed President and Mrs. George Washington moving into a very famous mansion—the White House. Quiet colors depicted the horse-drawn wagon piled high with household articles. Also shown were the White House servants, busy unloading it.

Trixie let out a deep breath. "It's beautiful!" she exclaimed. "Where did you find it?"

Mrs. Osilius beamed. "I was looking for a bargain," she replied, "and I found one right here in a little antique shop in Sleepyside. It just opened for business. I don't believe the owner realizes the true worth of this painting. He does know that it's old. He said it was painted by a famous artist in 1789, the year that our first President was elected."

"Did you tell him we'd buy it?" one of the other students asked.

"No," answered Mrs. Osilius. "But he's willing to sell it for the exact amount of money we have in our treasury. I told him I'd return with a check right after our meeting."

"I think we should return," Honey said slowly, "but with the police, not a check. Mrs. Osilius, I'm sorry to tell you this, but the dealer is trying to cheat us. It may be beautiful, but this painting is definitely a fake!"

What made Honey so sure?

HORSE THIEVES!

While at a horse show with Honey, Trixie was curious when a woman picked up a discarded program and then studied it intently, though she had one of her own. Then, when the woman left during the second event and looked around furtively before slipping that same program into a trash can, Trixie's curiosity became suspicion.

Two minutes after retrieving the program, Trixie raced to the security police and gasped, "They're trying to steal the Wheelers' horse, Lady!"

Can you crack the code and read the thieves' message?

CLASS SCHEDULE
SATURDAY

Class 2—Third level, Test 3—OPEN

Time			Name	
9:00	32	1	Bring It Home	Jeanette Elton
9:08	87		Que Suerte	Julio Mendez
9:16	49	4,5	Nobody's Fool	Robert T. Railer
9:24	25	½	Afterglow	Sandra Rosenberg
9:32	38	8	I Say, Old Chap	Rupert P. Hill, II
9:40	76		What a Riot	Stanley Bishop-Jones
9:48	75	1	Lady's Choice	Willy Jones
9:56	55		Morning Star	Cheryl Christiansen
10:04	19	2	Off Guard	Danny Ozowski
10:12	26		Jo-Jo-Jo	Harold Boehm
10:20	60		Chocolate Pie	Stacy Zimmerman
10:28	63		Bettor's Choice	Ming Hsu
10:36	54	3,4,5,6½	In and Out	O. F. "Itsy" Wayland
10:44	51		Milly	Mike Spencer

MISSING PARTNERS

Mart and his friend Bob Hubbell are always having "word" contests. They challenge each other to see who can finish word games like this pairing list first. Try to provide the missing partner for each of these words. Some of them are very easy. Some are not! What's your time score?

1. WASH and _ _ _ _
2. SHOES and _ _ _ _ _
3. DOLLARS and _ _ _ _ _
4. BREAD and _ _ _ _ _ _
5. LEWIS and _ _ _ _ _
6. HOOK and _ _ _
7. HEAD and _ _ _ _ _ _ _ _ _
8. LOCK and _ _ _
9. SPICK and _ _ _ _
10. SONG and _ _ _ _ _
11. NEEDLE and _ _ _ _ _ _
12. BALL and _ _ _
13. NIGHT and _ _ _ _
14. ODDS and _ _ _ _
15. HAMMER and _ _ _ _ _
16. PETER and _ _ _ _ _
17. BLACK and _ _ _ _ _
18. KNIFE and _ _ _ _
19. ROMULUS and _ _ _ _ _
20. BACK and _ _ _ _ _

21. HOOK and _ _ _ _ _ _
22. HAT and _ _ _ _
23. INS and _ _ _ _
24. CLOAK and _ _ _ _ _ _
25. BEAUTY and _ _ _ _ _ _ _ _
26. ACHES and _ _ _ _ _
27. BOOTS and _ _ _ _ _ _
28. OPEN and _ _ _ _
29. DAVID and _ _ _ _ _ _ _
30. SIXES and _ _ _ _ _ _
31. BUTTONS and _ _ _ _
32. SATIN and _ _ _ _
33. SHARPS and _ _ _ _ _
34. JACOB and _ _ _ _
35. GOLD and _ _ _ _ _ _
36. PEN and _ _ _
37. WIND and _ _ _ _
38. POTS and _ _ _ _
39. SALT and _ _ _ _ _ _
40. ADAM and _ _ _

PIRATES BOLD

"I didn't know this about treasure maps," Trixie told Honey.

"You didn't know what about treasure maps?" Honey asked. "Are you getting us into another mystery?"

"No. I'm just doing this quiz about pirates. Let's do it together."

"Okay," Honey agreed. "But don't expect me to know very many answers."

"You might be surprised," Trixie said. "Here goes."

1. What makes us suspect that Captain Kidd was not always clever about burying his treasure?

2. If a man was shanghaied in the days of piracy, where would he have been likely to wake up?

3. The buccaneers' flag is _____ in color, and on it usually appears a _____ and _____ or a _____.

4. Buccaneers are so called because of
   a. their method of drying meat.
   b. their bold ways.
   c. the type of ship they used.

5. Pirates are also called which of the following:
   a. rovers?   b. corsairs?
   c. picaroons?   d. freebooters?

6. If a pirate had a salmagundi, would he be likely to
   a. eat it?   b. toss it overboard?   c. bury it?

7. Was the captain usually the owner of a pirate ship?

8. What was a piece of eight?

9. Is it true that there is a list of treasure maps and charts in the Library of Congress?

10. Who was the pirate?

| Captain Kidd | Blackbeard (Edward Teach) | Henry Morgan | Jean Lafitte |

a. Which of these four took great pains to look so terrifying that often just his appearance frightened his victims away?

b. Which of the four helped to defend New Orleans?

c. Which was kidnapped when young, sold as a slave, became a famous buccaneer, and was arrested and taken to England—where he was made a knight and a deputy governor of Jamaica?

d. Which went to sea as a boy of thirteen and was an honest seaman until the king of England asked him to capture pirates?

GRIMM CASTLE

"What a great Halloween cookout this has been," Trixie said as she and her friends watched the glowing campfire. "The only thing that's missing tonight is a ghost."

"That's not true, Trix," Jim said slowly. "There *is* a ghost here. Maybe you guys can't see him, but I sure can. He's with me night and day now."

Honey gasped. "Why, Jim! Are you kidding?"

"It all began when we were in England," her brother said. "I—I wanted to explore the old ruins of Grimm Castle, even though we'd been warned to stay away. Everyone had told me about the ghost who haunted it. . . . Centuries ago, he'd been a prisoner in the castle dungeons. Later, his specter roamed the ruins. He'd be freed only if he found someone to give him a new home."

Mart stared. "How come I didn't know you went there?"

"I sneaked out late one night," Jim answered, "and took our rented English car. I locked the doors and rolled up the windows before I even started across the dark moors to Grimm Castle.

"I saw the ghost immediately! It was terrible! His clothes were in rags. Chains hung from his skinny wrists and ankles. He leaped toward the car and tried to get in. I could see a hideous wart that grew on his left cheekbone. 'Jim Frayne,' he moaned, 'I've been waiting for you. Now I have you in my power!' "

Di swallowed hard. "What did you do?"

"I tried to drive off," Jim cried, "but the car wouldn't move! I just knew I'd be stuck there to the end of my days! There was only one thing I could do—I unlocked the front door on the passenger side, and I let the ghost get in! As I drove away with him, all I could see out of the corner of my eye was that ghastly wart on the side of his face. 'I'll haunt you forever, Jim Frayne!' he shrieked. And he has!"

Everyone jumped as a log in the fire suddenly collapsed in a shower of sparks.

Trixie shivered. "What a wonderful Halloween story, Jim," she said. "You almost had me believing you—and you only made one little mistake."

What was the mistake Jim made?

STATE NAMES AND NICKNAMES

Mr. and Mrs. Wheeler, Honey's parents, have been all over the world, but when Honey gave them this quiz about just fifteen of the fifty United States, they missed several of them. Can you identify each of these fifteen states?

1. I'm the Show Me State, and my name means "muddy water."

2. My name was originally given to me by the Spanish conquistadors; people know me best as the Golden State.

3. James Oglethorpe named me after one of England's kings. I'm also nicknamed the Peach State.

4. My name was derived from the Russian version of an Eskimo word meaning "peninsula" or "great lands."

5. It is said that Ponce de Leon named me "Flowery Easter" on Easter Sunday, 1513. What am I called today?

6. The Chippewa Indians named me "Great Water." One of my borders is a lake with the same name.

7. I'm nicknamed the Pelican State, and part of my territory was named after a French king.

8. My name is a combination of the French words meaning "green" and "mountain."

9. I'm the Grand Canyon State.

10. My Indian name can be translated as "one who puts to sleep" or "beautiful land." I'm nicknamed the Hawkeye State.

11. Nobody knows for sure where the word **hoosier** came from, but I'm the Hoosier State.

12. I'm the smallest state, and a chicken is named after me.

13. A **sooner** is a person who settled on land in the early West before (sooner than) it was officially opened to settlers. My citizens are nicknamed Sooners.

14. The sea gull is my official state bird, but I'm a long way from the sea. I'm the Beehive State.

15. I'm called the First State because I was the first one to approve our Constitution. I'm also the northernmost Southern state—I bet you didn't know that!

STUMPERS

"Some of your quizzes really stumped me, Trixie," Jim said. "Maybe one of these will stump *you*."

1. It's February 1 in the year 2000. You want a horse to ride every day this month. How many horses will you need?

2. A great-grandfather said, as he looked around the room at all of his family, "Who's going to sit on the floor? I have just four chairs—and in this room are three fathers, one great-granddaughter, one daughter, two sons, two grandchildren, two grandfathers, and one great-grandfather. Will someone get some more chairs, please?"

   The daughter said, "But four chairs are exactly right."

   Was the daughter too young to count, or was the great-grandfather seeing folks who weren't there? Who was right?

45

THE
SAFE
ROBBER

1. HELP! STOP THAT MAN!

2. WHAT MAN? WHAT'S WRONG?

3. MY UNCLE'S BEEN ROBBED!

4. MAYBE THE THIEF LEFT SOME CLUES. TELL US WHAT HAPPENED.

5. MY UNCLE DOESN'T CARE HOW HE LIVES. HE ONLY CARES ABOUT MONEY.

6. HE'S IN THE HOSPITAL, SO I CAME TO SEE THAT EVERYTHING WAS ALL RIGHT HERE.

7. WHEN I OPENED THE FRONT DOOR, I SAW THE MAN DART INTO THE KITCHEN AND OUT THE KITCHEN DOOR. I STARTED TO CHASE HIM, BUT... YOU KNOW THE REST.

8. HONEY, CALL SERGEANT MOLINSON... AND TELL HIM WE HAVE THE THIEF!

HOW DID TRIXIE GUESS THAT THE NEPHEW WAS THE SAFE ROBBER?

THE MISSING WILL

Ever since Mr. Hartman had helped Trixie solve the Secret of the Unseen Treasure, they had become good friends. Now the friendly ex-policeman was telling her and Honey about a case he'd had in the Albany police force, to see if they could also solve it.

"A well-known photographer, Ned Smith, was an expert on wildlife. He never made mistakes in his work," Mr. Hartman was saying.

"I first heard about him after he died. According to his will, he left all his money and possessions to his niece, who was a friend of mine. Ned had been a suspicious old man who didn't trust either lawyers or banks. So he'd hidden the will somewhere in the house for safekeeping, but his niece couldn't find it. She told me that if the will didn't turn up, she'd be left homeless and penniless!"

"How awful!" Honey exclaimed. "What did you do?"

"It was logical that he'd put the will some-where in his study," Mr. Hartman said, "so I looked there first. The walls were lined with photographs. Each photograph was in a frame and had a hand-printed label. For instance, a photograph of a big brown bear had a label that said, 'Barney the bear can run twenty-five miles an hour.'"

"Barney the bear?" Trixie said with a big smile. "That's cute. What else did you see?"

"I saw photographs of a goldfish named Goldie, a pigeon named Homer, and a beautiful peacock, whose label said, 'Polly the peacock defends her nest.'"

"What furniture was in the study?" Honey asked.

"There was a big rolltop desk in one corner, two comfortable armchairs by the fireplace, a couple of lamps, and a number of low, two-shelf bookcases," Mr. Hartman replied.

"Did you ever find the will?" Honey asked.

Trixie giggled. "Of course he found the will, Honey. Ned Smith had left an obvious clue to its hiding place."

What was the clue Trixie noticed?

DOODLERS' NOODLERS

"Jim," asked Trixie, "what are all those doodles?"

Jim grinned at her and said, "I've been thinking. Is a picture really worth a thousand words? I doubt if mine are—but they are worth one, two, or three words. They're sports terms." He showed Trixie a sketch of a head with no features. "What does this say? It's a hockey term."

Trixie guessed it right away. "Face-off!" she said. "And that makes me think of one."

Soon they were both making sketches to be translated into sports terms. How many can you figure out?

(NOTE: Some terms may apply to more than one sport.)

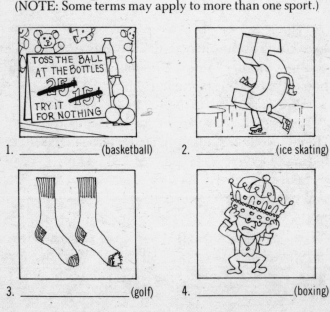

1. _____ (basketball)   2. _____ (ice skating)

3. _____ (golf)   4. _____ (boxing)

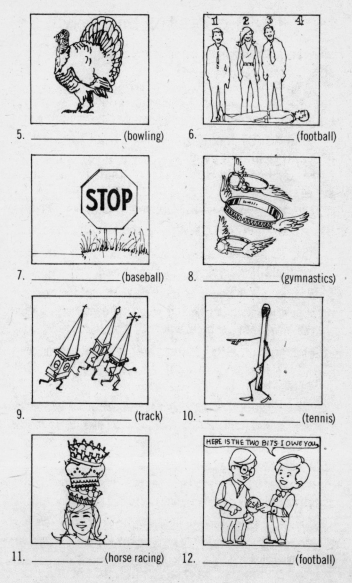

5. _____ (bowling)

6. _____ (football)

7. _____ (baseball)

8. _____ (gymnastics)

9. _____ (track)

10. _____ (tennis)

11. _____ (horse racing)

12. _____ (football)

LIZARDS AND LUCK

"Never let a lizard count your teeth," said Trixie solemnly.

"What!" Honey exclaimed. "I'd never stay around a lizard long enough to—" She stopped as Trixie laughed.

"That advice about lizards came from this quiz on luck and wishes. It even tells how to give your wishes extra chances of coming true—that is, if you're superstitious."

"I'm not," Honey said. "Not really. But, well, I could use a little help with wishes. . . ."

1. What terrible thing is supposed to happen if you let a lizard count your teeth? (Hint: If you keep your mouth closed, it can't happen.)

2. When you buy new shoes, what can you do to add to your chances of bringing yourself a little extra good luck? (Hint: Right is hardly ever wrong when it comes to luck.)

3. What should be said to a four-leaf clover to make sure it will do its part in bringing you fame, wealth, honor, and health? (Hint: Counting helps here.)

4. Where is the place to put nine autumn leaves if you want to be lucky all winter? (Hint: It's a place you aren't likely to see in your dreams, even though it may be very near.)

5. If you want to give your wish every chance of coming true, what is one important thing you must **not** do? (Hint: This may be the hardest part.)

6. If a ghost should happen to float into the vicinity, what are four words to say to persuade it to go elsewhere? (Hint: Ghosts hate prying questions.)

7. If you think witches might be a bother, what is a good way to stop them from entering your room or house? (Hint: Witches feel compelled to count.)

8. If you want a black cat to bring you **good** luck, what should you do? (Hint: If you like cats, this is good for you **and** the black cat.)

9. If you see a beetle waving its legs, how can you bring yourself good luck? (Hint: It will also be lucky for the beetle.)

10. After you have studied for exams, what can you do with the books to bring good luck? (Hint: You might do this anyway, without even thinking.)

ONCE IS TOO MUCH

"Look at this funny old recipe," Honey told Trixie. "It fell out of an ancient book in our library. It sounds like a perfectly awful salad, doesn't it?"

Trixie took the faded paper covered with spidery handwriting and began reading.

6 green potatoes, sliced	⅔ lb. rhubarb leaves
¼ cup castor beans	1 doz. buttercups
10 Destroying Angel mushrooms	1 tsp. hemlock
	apple seeds (garnish)

"It's a concoction I wouldn't want to have very often!" Honey giggled.

Trixie disagreed. "This is something you wouldn't want to have even once!" she declared.

Why did Trixie say that?

The Mystery of the Missing Wallet

"My wallet's been stolen!" Mark Wolfe exclaimed, bursting through the doorway of his fourth-hour class at Sleepyside Junior-Senior High School.

For the ten minutes before Mark's entrance, the students had been working silently on a difficult algebra problem the teacher had written on the board. But immediately after his announcement, their silence changed to surprised gasps and murmurs. A theft in their school was shocking in itself; the fact that the victim was Mark Wolfe, whose friendly and outgoing personality made him one of the best-liked boys in the Sleepyside school, was even worse.

Trixie Belden was the only student who remained silent after Mark spoke. But her silence wasn't from lack of interest. To her, a stolen wallet meant a mystery to be solved, and mysteries were the most interesting things in the world to Trixie. So, while her classmates murmured among themselves, Trixie sat in rigid silence, waiting for Mark to share the details of the theft with the class.

Unfortunately, Trixie's attentiveness was noticed by Jerry Vanderhoef, the school's most notorious troublemaker. "Hey, Mark!" Jerry shouted above the other students' whispers. "Just give the facts to Supersleuth Trixie, here! She'll solve the mystery faster than the rest of the class can solve this algebra problem!" He looked at Trixie, his upper lip curled in a sneer as he added, "Faster than *she* can solve the algebra problem, too!"

Trixie blushed to the roots of her sandy hair and lowered her head to stare unseeingly at her math book. Jerry's sarcastic reference to her detective work was embarrassing, but the reference to her problems in math, made in front of the whole class—and the teacher—was downright humiliating. She found herself blinking back tears of anger.

The teacher realized that he was losing control

of his class. After making sure that Mark had reported the loss to the principal, he turned to the blackboard and began leading the class through the algebra problem.

The difficulties of algebra soon distracted Trixie from both Jerry's cruel remark and the missing wallet, but as soon as the bell rang, she gathered up her books and hurried after Mark.

The boy was standing in the hallway, surrounded by curious classmates. Trixie hesitated when she saw Jerry Vanderhoef in the group. She wanted to ask Mark where and when the wallet had been stolen, but she didn't want to risk another rude remark. She gave Jerry an icy stare. He returned it with his well-practiced sneer. "See ya later," he said to Mark, turning abruptly to leave and almost knocking tiny, dark-haired Carol Aronson over in the process.

"Excuse me," Carol said shyly as Jerry walked away without pausing.

It's easy to tell that Carol's new in school, Trixie thought, shaking her head in disgust at Jerry's rudeness. *If she'd been around long enough to get to know that guy, she wouldn't apologize to him for bumping into her.* Then Trixie turned her attention to Mark Wolfe. "How did it happen, Mark?" she asked.

"I was standing at my locker right before class," he said, "when Greg Kabara came over and asked me if I had a postage stamp. I took my wallet out of my back pocket and pulled out the stamp folder. Then I put the wallet on top of my locker so I could pull out a stamp." Mark spoke slowly, staring over Trixie's head as he visualized what had happened. "Greg and I got to talking about one thing and another, and I guess I just absentmindedly stuck the stamp folder back in my pocket where the wallet had been, picked up my books, shut my locker, and walked down the hall with him. How dumb can you get?"

Trixie grinned wryly. "That sounds perfectly normal to me," she said. "At least, it's the kind of thing I do all the time. I suppose my brother Mart would argue that that proves it *isn't* normal. But when did you notice that the wallet wasn't in your pocket?"

"Just before I got to algebra class," Mark told her. "I ran back to my locker as fast as I could, but the wallet was gone. Then I ran to the office to see if someone had turned it in. No one had."

"How much money was in the wallet?" Trixie asked.

Mark grinned sheepishly. "None. I have a part-time job after school. Today is payday, so, as usual, I'm down to loose change until I cash my check. But that wallet had my driver's license, my library card, my Social Security card, class pictures of all my friends—" Mark shrugged helplessly. "I'd really like to get it back."

"Of course you would," Trixie agreed. "And I think your chances are pretty good. If the thief is someone from school, he won't risk keeping the wallet and having you spot him with it. I think we should get some people together after school and search. We'll probably find the wallet in the building somewhere."

Mark Wolfe began to look more and more relieved as Trixie spoke, and he was smiling as he told her, "I like that theory, Trixie. In fact, that wallet has my initials on it, which makes it even more likely that the thief won't keep it. I'll ask some people to help during my last two classes, and we'll meet you at the front door after school."

The "search party" that gathered that afternoon in front of the school was a fairly large one. Trixie had enlisted the help of the Bob-Whites of the Glen, a semisecret club that Trixie had founded together with her older brothers, Mart and Brian, her friend Honey Wheeler, and Honey's adopted brother, Jim. Di Lynch and Dan Mangan had later joined the club, which was devoted to helping others, as well as to having fun. Mark had also spread the word among his many friends.

Still, an hour and a half later, even Trixie had to admit defeat. "We've searched every inch of the building," she said dejectedly. "The wallet just isn't here. I'm sorry, Mark."

"Sorry for what, Trixie?" Mark asked, keeping his tone light, although his disappointment showed on his face. "You and your friends just spent a lot of time trying to find my wallet. You should be accepting my thanks, not offering me apologies."

"My sympathetic sibling seizes the sorrows of all who surround her," Mart Belden said. His tone was teasing, but there was sympathy in his eyes, too.

"Speaking of sympathy," Brian added, "I think we should show some for Moms, who's had our rambunctious younger brother to herself for the past two hours."

"Gleeps!" Trixie exclaimed. "That's right! We've got to go now. See you tomorrow, Mark."

Calling their good-byes, the Bob-Whites piled into their club station wagon.

"I'm really surprised that we didn't find that wallet," Trixie muttered as they turned down Crabtree Lane.

She was even more surprised the next afternoon when Carol Aronson walked into algebra class a few minutes before the bell, went directly to Mark Wolfe's desk, and said, "Here's your wallet."

Mark's jaw dropped in surprise. Then he broke

into a wide grin as he took the wallet from her and looked through it. "Everything's here!" he said. "Where did you find it?"

Carol cleared her throat nervously before she spoke. "I—I heard you talking to Trixie after class yesterday. I heard her say that you should search the building because the thief would probably throw the wallet away. I thought that the thief might try to get rid of it on his way home after school. So when we finished searching *inside* the building, I looked around *outside* and found it in the trash can at the corner by the stoplight."

"Great thinking!" Mark exclaimed, causing Carol to blush and lower her head to stare at the floor. "Listen," he said, "I can't let this go unrewarded. I'd like to give you a hundred dollars . . . but would you settle for a Coke at Wimpy's after school?"

Carol Aronson looked as astonished as Mark had when she'd handed him the wallet. "Y-You don't have to— I mean, I didn't expect—"

"I know I don't have to," Mark said, "and I know you didn't expect. But I insist. Let's meet at the main entrance right after school."

Trixie suddenly realized that she had been staring at Mark and Carol, and that the look on her face probably registered disappointment and disbelief that it had been Carol Aronson, not the

Bob-Whites, who had found the wallet. She turned away to see Jerry Vanderhoef smirking at her. She lowered her head and braced herself for another sarcastic remark, but just then the teacher hurried into the room, and the bell signaled the beginning of the class.

When she finally was able to talk to the rest of the Bob-Whites, she found that none of them shared her disbelief.

"There's something about Carol's story that just doesn't ring true," Trixie protested.

"Could it be that your erstwhile azure ocular orbs have succumbed to verdure?" Mart asked.

"I'm not green-eyed with jealousy, if that's what you mean," Trixie said hotly. "But look: Carol said she got the idea of looking *outside* the school building from what I was saying after class about looking *inside*. So why didn't she say something right then, while we were all standing in the hallway? And we were all inside the school for a whole hour and a half. If her super theory led her right to his wallet, why didn't she bring it to Mark right then, instead of waiting until this afternoon in algebra class?"

"Calm down, Trixie," Brian said firmly. "How do you know Carol came up with her theory immediately? It could have occurred to her anytime before school let out—or even later, while we were searching the building. And I doubt that she told Mark that her 'super theory led her right to his wallet.' She could have searched a long time after we went home."

"Well, why didn't she ask us to help her search outside?" Trixie asked.

"Carol is still very new here, and just from seeing her in the halls, I'd say she's shy—painfully shy," Dan Mangan said. "I still remember what it was like to be new at Sleepyside Junior-Senior High, and I can tell you that a much more outgoing person than Carol would find it hard to march up to a group of strangers and ask them to help *her* search outside after all that time."

"Besides, Trixie," Di Lynch added, "you can't deny that Carol Aronson did solve the mystery. You saw her give Mark the wallet."

"What if she found the wallet without solving the mystery?" Trixie asked. Seeing her friends' blank looks, she explained. "I mean, she could have found the wallet by chance, maybe on her way home, maybe a few blocks from school, and then invented her theory afterward."

Mart shook his head. "I would recommend that you desist, Beatrix, before your admirable trait of perseverance is transmogrified into the unattractive posture of perseverating."

"Mart is right," Brian said. "It's natural for you to be disappointed that you didn't solve this mystery. But don't let your disappointment turn to sour grapes. You've solved other, more impressive mysteries before, and you will again. Let Carol take credit for this one."

Trixie sighed. "You're both right, as usual, Brian. I guess I've started to think of myself as the world's greatest detective. It's hard to admit that I got beat out of solving this one. But I just did, and that's all there is to it."

The next noon, when Trixie met Honey for lunch, Honey didn't even say hello before she blurted, "Oh, Trixie, someone stole Michelle Martin's new leather coat!"

"When, Honey?" Trixie demanded. "How?"

"Michelle always gets to school about half an hour early, because her father drops her off on his way to work in Croton. There are several other students who get here early, and they all go to the cafeteria to study."

Trixie grinned in spite of the seriousness of the conversation. "I've come in early for make-up tests and walked past the cafeteria. If those kids are studying for anything, it must be a class in giggling that I don't know about."

Honey let out a giggle of her own. "Michelle explained what happened to our first-hour class, including the teacher. I guess maybe I'm repeating her story a little too closely to the way she told it."

"Anyway, what's the rest of the story?" Trixie

asked, growing serious once again.

"Well, Michelle's locker is on the third floor, right next to the first-hour class I have with her. So she goes directly to the cafeteria when her dad drops her off, then goes upstairs to her locker right before class. This morning was the first morning she'd worn her coat, since we've had such a warm fall, and—"

"—And," Trixie interrupted, "she and her friends left the cafeteria, lost in conversation, and Michelle was all the way upstairs before she realized that she'd left her coat in the cafeteria. She ran to get it, but it was gone. Am I right?"

Honey nodded solemnly. "That's exactly right, Trixie—and it's exactly like the theft of Mark's wallet."

Trixie frowned. "First Mark's wallet, now Michelle's coat. Two thefts, so close together. . . ."

"It's beginning to look as though there *is* a thief among us," Honey said softly. "And, oh, Trixie, in a school this size, it's almost bound to be someone we know."

The girls looked at each other in worried silence for a moment, then Trixie turned and slammed her locker shut. "Let's go talk to Michelle. Maybe she can tell us something else that will help us catch the thief."

But all Michelle could tell them was that no one had been in the cafeteria that morning who wasn't usually there and that they had all left at the same time to go to their lockers or to their first class.

"How long before class did you leave?" Trixie asked.

"About ten minutes," Michelle replied.

"That would be plenty of time for someone to sneak into the cafeteria and take the coat," Honey said.

"It would," Trixie agreed, "but why would someone sneak into the cafeteria ten minutes before school starts? Unless—"

"Unless they knew my coat was there!" Michelle exclaimed. "That's what you were going to say, isn't it? You think that one of my friends went back to the cafeteria and stole my coat!"

"There's a strong argument for suspecting one of your friends in the cafeteria," Trixie said. "But there's just as strong an argument against it. Your leather coat would be even more conspicuous than Mark's wallet, especially if it were being worn by someone who sees you every morning."

Michelle and Honey looked relieved for a moment, then Honey frowned again. "The thief might not keep the coat. He—or she—could give it away or sell it someplace."

"Gleeps!" Trixie said. "I hadn't thought of

that." She sighed. "We'd better sit down and eat lunch. Sometimes I think better on a full stomach. We'll get your coat back, Michelle," Trixie promised.

As she and Honey went over to tell the other Bob-Whites about the theft, Trixie looked around the lunchroom at her schoolmates. How could one of these people, most of whom she'd been in school with for years, possibly be a thief? she wondered.

Suddenly Trixie found herself gazing across the cafeteria directly into the brown eyes of Carol Aronson. Carol started and lowered her gaze, then quickly gathered her things and hurried from the room.

For the first time, Trixie noticed that Carol had been sitting alone at the table next to Michelle Martin's. *I bet she was eavesdropping*, Trixie thought, *trying to overhear clues that she can use to find the coat.*

"What's the matter, Trixie?" Brian asked, calling her attention back to them.

"It's painful to think that one of our schoolmates is a thief," Honey supplied, voicing her own concern.

"That's part of it," Trixie agreed. "It's also painful to think that I have no idea who's doing the stealing. If anything else is stolen, everybody'll start to suspect their own friends, just as

Michelle is beginning to. Nobody will trust any-body else anymore. I don't want that to happen, and yet I haven't a single clue to use to catch the thief." Trixie sighed heavily.

"Give yourself some time, Trix," Jim said. "You'll come up with the answer. You always have." He smiled at her with such warm reassur-ance that Trixie felt herself beginning to blush.

"The main problem," Brian said reflectively, "is that there doesn't seem to be a pattern to the thefts. First a boy's wallet is stolen from a second-floor locker, then a girl's coat is stolen from the first-floor cafeteria. The wallet would have been taken for its contents, but the coat would have to have been taken for its own sake. The only thing the two items have in common is that they're both made of leather. It doesn't make any sense."

"Speaking of not making sense . . ." Mart mut-tered, looking across the cafeteria, where a com-motion had erupted.

Jerry Vanderhoef and his friends, Bill Wright and Mike Larson, had taken their lunch bags to the row of garbage cans that stood along one row of the cafeteria. But instead of just depositing the bags, they had begun an impromptu game of basketball. Each took a turn tossing his bag at one of the cans, while the other two alternated cheers and catcalls. Because they were tossing the bags from behind their backs and under their legs, they missed repeatedly, and the game continued until the cafeteria monitor walked toward them. Then they dropped the bags into the garbage and sauntered away.

The Bob-Whites collected their things and walked to the door of the cafeteria, arriving at the same time as Jerry Vanderhoef.

"Hey, Supersleuth Trixie," the boy said loudly, "I heard there's another mystery for you to solve. Or are you letting that new kid handle all your cases for you?"

Trixie felt her face growing hot with anger, but, feeling Jim's hand on her arm, she forced herself to say nothing, and Jerry turned his back on the Bob-Whites and walked away.

"He's really got it in for you, Trixie, hasn't he?" Dan said.

Trixie shrugged. "I can take it, I guess. I don't enjoy it, but I don't think enough of Jerry Vanderhoef to let his criticism bother me."

"Good girl," Jim murmured approvingly as the Bob-Whites reached the end of the hallway and went to their separate classes.

Trixie found herself smiling contentedly as she walked down the hall. *See there?* she thought. *Why should I let someone I don't care about bother me, when just two words from someone I respect, like Jim, can make my whole day?*

Lying in bed that night, Trixie found her attention once again turning to the thefts at school, wondering if they would continue and if she could discover the clue she needed to solve them.

"The problem, as Brian said, is that the thefts are senseless," she muttered to herself in the darkness. "As senseless as the rowdy things that Jerry Vanderhoef and his friends do."

Suddenly Trixie sat up in bed as she remembered what Dan had said to her about Jerry: "He's really got it in for you, hasn't he, Trixie?"

"I've always known that I'm not Jerry Vanderhoef's best friend," Trixie muttered to herself again, "but what if he really hates me? What if he's committing these thefts just to upset me, knowing that I can't solve them because they're so senseless?"

Trixie sat and thought for a moment, then lay back down. "That's pretty farfetched, I guess," she said to herself.

But her mind kept working the theory over. Mark Wolfe's locker was close to Jerry Vanderhoef's, so if Jerry had been at his locker when Mark left his wallet, he would have been able to pick it up without attracting attention—and have plenty of time to get to algebra class.

Maybe he'd intended to return the wallet to Mark during class, then came up with the revenge idea when he saw how interested I was in what Mark was saying, Trixie thought. *Well, it may be a farfetched theory, but it's the only lead I've come up with. I'll just have to get to school early tomorrow morning and ask Michelle if she noticed Jerry hanging around this morning when her coat was stolen.* With that, she rolled over and drifted off to sleep.

The next morning, Trixie coaxed Brian into giving her a ride to school in his jalopy, arriving at school fifteen minutes ahead of the bus. As she neared the cafeteria, the sounds of laughter and talking seemed louder than usual. *I guess Michelle and her friends have recovered from the theft faster than I have*, she thought.

She went in and sat down next to Michelle. "I want to talk to you about your coat," she began.

"Oh, hi, Trixie," Michelle said. "Look! I got it back!" She held up the coat. "Carol found it and gave it to me right after school. I didn't even have to tell my parents it had been missing!"

Carol Aronson smiled shyly at Trixie. "I couldn't help overhearing something you said to Michelle yesterday, about how conspicuous that leather coat would be. I tried to imagine how the thief would even get it out of the school. I guess that was still in the back of my mind when I was walking to my last class yesterday. When I saw a big paper bag tucked into a corner just outside the cafeteria, something made me stop and look inside. And there was Michelle's coat!" Carol looked surprised at the lengthy speech she'd just made and lowered her eyes to the open book in front of her.

"Carol thinks that the thief took the coat, shoved it into the bag, and put the bag in the corner until after school, when he could retrieve it and leave the building without being noticed. Wasn't it clever of her to think of that?" Michelle asked.

Trixie swallowed hard. "It—it certainly was clever," she stammered. "Well—congratulations." She got up and hurried out of the cafeteria.

The second stolen object had been found, too. By Carol! But Carol hadn't found the thief. . . . Trixie was halfway down the hall before she realized that she'd forgotten to ask Michelle about Jerry. *Maybe it's just as well*, she thought. *With all those people around, I could have raised suspicions about him. That's something I've got to avoid until I have more proof that he's the thief.*

Trixie needed to confide in someone, though, so she asked Honey to meet her that evening after dinner.

In the privacy of the clubhouse, Trixie told her best friend and partner in the future Belden-Wheeler Detective Agency about her suspicions.

Honey sat in silence for a few moments, weighing the evidence in her mind. "Their lockers being close together really isn't much to go on, Trixie," she said. "I don't like Jerry Vanderhoef very well, either, but I don't want to risk making his reputation even worse by accusing him falsely of being the thief."

Trixie sighed. "I know it, Honey. We need more evidence. And Carol Aronson is keeping us from getting it."

"Oh, Trixie," Honey said reprovingly, "don't tell me you're still feeling jealous of poor, shy Carol!"

"Of course I'm not," Trixie said defensively. Then she sighed again. "Well, maybe I am a little jealous. But returning stolen goods to the owners isn't the same thing as solving the crimes."

"That's true," Honey agreed. "I'm really glad Mark and Michelle got their things back. I'm glad Carol has made some new friends, too, but we really aren't any closer to catching the thief."

Trixie nodded. "Now if Carol had left that bag where it was and come back right after class—" Trixie stopped in midsentence and excitedly grabbed Honey by the shoulders. "That's it!" she exclaimed.

"What's it?" Honey asked. Her hazel eyes sparkled with excitement. She knew from past experience that when Trixie shouted "That's it!" they were on the verge of solving a mystery.

"The only way to prove that Jerry is the thief is to catch him red-handed," Trixie said.

"Of course," Honey replied. "But how can we do that if we don't know what he's going to steal next—and where?"

"He's going to steal a wristwatch from the third desk of the fifth row of room two-oh-eight between fourth and fifth periods tomorrow," Trixie said triumphantly.

"How can you possibly know that?" Honey asked. "Don't tell me you're able to predict the future!"

"I can in this case," Trixie said, "because it's my desk in algebra class, and I'm going to leave the watch there. We have a test tomorrow, and I always take my watch off and lay it on my desk during a test so that I can keep track of the time I have left. Tomorrow, I'll gather up my books but leave the watch on the desk. Then I'll wait around the corner, where I can see into the classroom without being seen. Anyone who sees me in the hall will think I'm just waiting for a friend. It's perfect, Honey!"

Trixie's friend shook her head. "It's far from being perfect, Trixie," she said. "First of all, if Jerry Vanderhoef isn't the thief, the whole experiment will be for nothing. And even if he is, if something goes wrong—like someone distracting you in the hallway at the time—you could lose your watch without catching him red-handed."

Trixie shrugged. "We have to do something, and we have to do it before the thief disrupts the entire school."

Honey hesitated. "All right. Let's try it. I'll be just down the hall, in case you need help."

The next afternoon, Trixie walked to her desk, sat down, put her books under the seat, and took off her watch. She placed it deliberately on the corner of her desk and wondered fleetingly if she'd ever see it again once she left it. Smiling wryly, she thought, *If Jerry gets away with it, maybe Carol Aronson will find it and return it to me.*

She took one of the test papers from the stack that was passed down the row and began to work. As soon as the bell rang, Trixie gathered her books and left, taking up her position just outside the door.

The classroom emptied rapidly, and finally Jerry Vanderhoef came into view. Trixie caught her breath as she saw him glance at her watch and start toward it. Then he turned and walked out of the classroom. He paused as he passed Trixie in the hallway and said, "Hey, Supersleuth, you left your watch in there. I was going to bring it to you, but I figured you'd have me arrested on the spot as class thief.''

Trixie let out her breath in a disappointed sigh. The experiment had failed. Either Jerry was not the thief, or he had realized that the watch was a trap and passed it by.

Honey came up just as Trixie started back into the room for the watch. They froze in their tracks, then ducked back into the doorway as they saw Carol Aronson slip over to Trixie's desk. Carol looked around furtively, snatched Trixie's watch, and slipped it into her purse.

A sick feeling descended on Trixie as the truth came to her. "Carol," she said, her voice sounding unnatural in the now-empty classroom. "You—did you take Mark's wallet, too—and Michelle's coat?"

Startled, Carol Aronson stared at Trixie, then swallowed hard. Nodding silently, she held out the watch to Trixie, her eyes wide with fear.

Trixie didn't take her eyes from Carol's face. "I think we'd better talk, Carol. Will you meet us at the bike rack after school?"

Carol nodded again. Trixie took the watch from her still-outstretched hand and silently left the room with Honey.

After school, Carol was waiting at the bike rack, looking tiny and frail, when Trixie and Honey arrived. She forced herself to look up when Trixie asked, "Why did you do it, Carol?"

"It—it all just *happened*," she said helplessly. "I saw a wallet on top of a locker. I picked it up, looked inside, and saw Mark Wolfe's driver's license. I took it with me, intending to give it back to him before class. Then he came in late and said someone had *stolen* the wallet. I—I panicked. I decided to return it to him after class, but then there was a crowd around him, and you were talking about it as a theft, and I realized that returning the wallet then, after not saying anything for a whole hour, would look even worse. So I kept it.

"That night, I tried to figure out what to do. Then I remembered what you'd said about the thief throwing the wallet away, and I made up that story about finding it in the trash can."

I had that part of it right, anyway, Trixie thought. "And Michelle's coat?" she asked.

Tears welled in Carol's eyes. "Please try to understand," she said. "I've been miserable since I transferred to Sleepyside this fall. It's always been hard for me to make friends, and here, where everyone has known everyone else for practically their whole lives, it's been impossible. Then I made up the story about finding Mark's wallet, and all of a sudden I found myself in a booth at Wimpy's with one of the most popular kids in school. It was the first time anybody'd paid any attention to me since I came here."

"So when Michelle forgot her coat, you decided to get more attention," Honey said.

Carol nodded. "You want to hear something funny?" she asked, a bitter edge in her voice. "When you asked Michelle about her coat, she said everyone had left the cafeteria that morning at the same time. But I had stayed behind. I've been in that cafeteria every morning since school started, and they've never even *noticed* me. So of course, no one noticed me taking the coat to my locker. I just kept it there until after school."

Carol paused, and a silence descended, broken only by the sounds of football practice coming from the field behind the school. At last she asked, "What are you going to do to me?"

"Well," Trixie said slowly, "you didn't really steal anything, I guess. You just took a little longer than necessary to return things."

"And we understand, now, how it happened," Honey added. "Really, the only thing you did wrong was to make up those stories about finding things, and making up stories isn't always a crime." Honey smiled. "If it were, Trixie and I would be behind bars by now."

Trixie laughed. "I'll say we would! But making up stories isn't the only thing you did wrong, Carol. You also underestimated yourself and the kids at Sleepyside. We're not as closed to outsiders as you make us sound, and you're not so worthless that you have to make up stories to make friends."

"I know that, now," Carol said. "Everybody has been friendly since I made those first steps. I just wish those first steps hadn't been lies."

"The important thing," Trixie told her, "is for you to take it from here, to work at making friends instead of letting yourself be miserable."

"I will," Carol said sincerely.

"I want you to promise us that someday, when you feel a little more comfortable with Mark and Michelle, you'll tell them what you did," Trixie said. "If you'll promise us that, we'll promise not to tell anyone else about this."

Fear leaped into Carol's eyes, but a look of determination soon replaced it. "I—I will," she promised.

"Trixie, we'll have to run if we're going to catch the school bus!" Honey said. "See you tomorrow, Carol."

"See you tomorrow," Carol said, making that statement, too, sound like a promise.

Honey and Trixie hurried to their favorite seats at the back of the bus. "Time will help Carol find a lot of friends here," Honey said.

"Yes," Trixie agreed thoughtfully. Then she grinned impishly at her best friend. "And if we're lucky, Honey, time will also help us find another mystery to solve."

COUNT-ATHON

Trixie solved several mysteries while working on fund-raising drives for charities such as UNICEF. Ms. Dupuis, Trixie's math teacher, promised her ten cents for every square she could find in the diagram below. If Trixie found them all, how much money would Ms. Dupuis give her for charity?

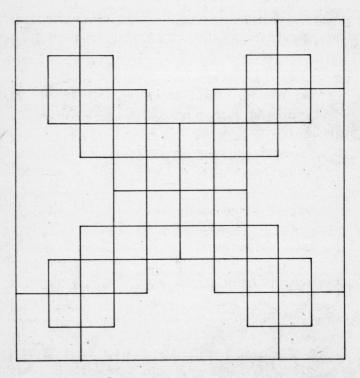

IT'S TRUE ... IT'S FALSE ... OH, I GIVE UP!

"I'll bet you can't get through this quiz without becoming discombobulated!" Mart challenged Trixie. "It's supposed to mix you up, but if you do exactly what it says, maybe you won't get any more wrong than I did."

"Oh, is that so!" Trixie retorted. "We'll just see about that!"

Here is the quiz. Trixie answered just one question incorrectly. (Mart never told his score!)

	YES	NO
1. Answer this wrong: Does a cube have six sides?	—	—
2. Answer this correctly: Is Milwaukee on the eastern shore of Lake Michigan?	—	—
3. Answer this wrong: Is the term **slalom** associated with skiing?	—	—
4. Answer this correctly: Was Daniel Boone a famous pioneer in Illinois?	—	—
5. Answer this wrong: Can the swift fly almost two hundred miles an hour?	—	—
6. Answer this wrong: Is it true that the Caspian Sea is not the largest inland sea?	—	—
7. Answer this wrong: Was **Sputnik** the first satellite to orbit the earth?	—	—
8. Answer this correctly: Is a podiatrist a specialist in the care of children?	—	—
9. Answer this correctly: Is it true that a galley is not an ancient boat?	—	—
10. Answer this wrong: Is Glasgow a city in Ireland?	—	—

TROUBLE IN THE DESERT

5. YOU'RE NOT LOST. THE HIGHWAY'S JUST ON THE OTHER SIDE OF THAT RISE. YOU CAN'T MISS IT.

6. SURE I LIVE ALONE. WHY?

WE JUST WANT TO WARN YOU THAT A ROBBER'S LOOSE AROUND HERE, AND HE'S ARMED.

7. HURRY!

8. WHY ARE YOU SO CERTAIN THAT THE MAN IN THE CABIN IS THE ROBBER, TRIXIE?

THAT SURE ISN'T HIS CABIN!

HOW DID TRIXIE KNOW?

THE
DISAPPEARING
DIAMONDS

"I hear you kids are good at figuring things out," said Mr. Morton. The jeweler sat in the Beldens' living room and talked to Trixie and her brothers. "Maybe you can help me.

"Today a man came into my shop and said he wanted to buy a diamond ring for his fiancée. I showed him what I had, and I had some very nice ones. He said that he couldn't decide and that he'd be back later and bring his fiancée with him.

"After he went out, I started to put away the tray of rings. Four of them were missing! The guy must have palmed four of the biggest ones!"

"Wow!" said Mart Belden. "Did he get away with them?"

"I'm afraid so, but I don't know how. I got his license number as he drove away, and the police stopped him before he reached the edge of town. They searched him and his car. No rings! Nothing!"

"He probably passed the diamonds to a confederate," said Brian.

Mr. Morton shook his head. "It doesn't seem likely. He's a known criminal, and he's a loner. He's never worked with another crook."

Mr. Morton sighed. Trixie felt sorry for him. His shop was just a small place sandwiched between a dress shop and the post office, but it contained lovely, precious things.

Suddenly Trixie had an idea. "Where's your crook now?" she asked Mr. Morton.

The jeweler shrugged. "The police had to let him go. There wasn't any evidence to hold him."

"Do they know where he lives?" Trixie asked.

"Sure. He's an ex-con. He reports to a parole officer."

"If there's a detective at his place tomorrow, the evidence will show up," said Trixie. Then she explained her hunch to Mr. Morton.

Can you guess what it was?

HORSES AND HORSE RACING

Six-year-old Bobby Belden made up three of the questions in this quiz about horses and horse racing. It won't be hard to recognize which ones are his.

1. The height of a horse is measured in
    a. feet.   b. yards.   c. hands.   d. shoes.

2. The first jockey to win more than five million dollars in one year was
    a. Steve Cauthen.   b. Eddie Arcaro.
    c. Willie Shoemaker.   d. Bill Hartack.

3. The fine lady in Banbury Cross, who wore rings on her fingers and bells on her toes, rode a
    a. cockhorse.   b. painted horse.
    c. white horse.   d. pony.

4. The youngest jockey (nine years ten months) ever to race was
    a. Willie Shoemaker.   b. Jimmy Taylor.
    c. Steve Cauthen.   d. Frank Wootten.

5. The oldest jockey (eighty years) ever to race was
    a. Willie Shoemaker.   b. Levi Barlingame.
    c. Frank Wootten.   d. Bill Hartack.

6. Young horses of both sexes under one year of age are called
    a. fillies.   b. colts.   c. geldings.   d. foals.

7. A horse that is a good distance runner is called a
    a. springer.   b. sprinter.
    c. router.   d. superhorse.

8. Harness racing involves horses with
   a. a special strap.   b. full blinders on.
   c. one of two gaits, pacing or trotting.
   d. at least four years of racing experience.

9. Mice are turned into horses in
   a. **Cinderella.**   b. **Black Beauty.**
   c. **Snow White.**   d. **Puss in Boots.**

10. The first horse race in the United States was held in
    the state of
    a. New York.   b. Virginia.
    c. Massachusetts.   d. Kentucky.

11. Which of the following is **not** a part of a horse's
    anatomy?
    a. withers   b. fetlock   c. crest   d. muzzle

12. Racing's "Triple Crown" consists of three races.
    Which one of these is **not** included?
    a. Kentucky Derby   b. Preakness
    c. Belmont Stakes   d. Hawthorne Royale

13. A horse race over a course of obstructions is called a
    a. hedgehop.   b. steeplechase.
    c. fox hunt.   d. harness race.

14. In the poem **Thanksgiving Day,** where was the horse
    going when it went "Over the river and through the
    wood"?
    a. out to old Aunt Mary's
    b. to grandfather's house
    c. to grandmother's house
    d. home again, home again

15. A Quarter Horse got its name because it
    a. weighs about a quarter ton.
    b. runs very fast for about a quarter mile.
    c. can make a quarter turn easily in order to
       cut a cow from a herd.
    d. has a life span of a quarter century.

THE MYSTERIOUS VALENTINE

When Trixie received the following valentine card, she wrinkled her nose at first, mystified to see a map of her neighborhood. Then a blush spread over her face as she realized whom the valentine was from and what she was supposed to do next. Can you figure it out?

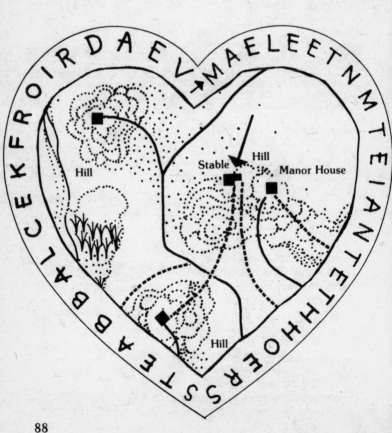

THE CASE OF
THE BAFFLING BANK BANDIT

Hooligan Harry, Gary the Goon, Bill the Bruiser, and Mean Mike Madison are the suspects in a bank robbery that Trixie is investigating. She has these clues:

1. All of the suspects are ex-convicts, and two of the ex-convicts were partners in crime before being sent to prison.

2. In prison, Gary the Goon first met the guilty suspect, who had been Hooligan Harry's partner.

3. Mean Mike Madison has never met Bill the Bruiser, although they served time at the same prison.

4. Bill the Bruiser never had a partner.

Who is the guilty suspect?

THE MYSTERY OF
THE GRITTY GRADES

Trixie, Honey, and Di are all taking English, algebra, and social studies at Sleepyside Junior-Senior High School. Two of the girls got C's in English last semester, and the other girl got an A. One of the two who got C's in English got a B in algebra; the other two got C's. One of the two who got a C in algebra also had a C in social studies, and the other two had B's. Honey's lowest grade was in algebra, and Di got the same grade in all three courses.

What grades did each of the girls receive?

89

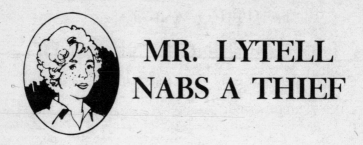

MR. LYTELL
NABS A THIEF

It was a beautiful August afternoon when Trixie slid to the ground from her horse's back. She looped Lady's reins loosely over a low-hanging branch outside Mr. Lytell's General Store.

When she led the rest of the Bob-Whites into the store, what a sight met their eyes! Mr. Lytell was wrestling with a young man near the baked goods, and the store was a mess!

"Help me!" Mr. Lytell yelled. "This is the crook who held me up last month! Something told me he'd be back to try again, and now I've got him! One of you kids call Sergeant Molinson and tell him to come quick!"

As Di hurried over to the phone, Jim and Dan each got a secure hold on the young man so that he couldn't get away. Stepping back, Mr. Lytell gingerly touched his jaw, where the young man had struck him while struggling to free himself.

"Are you all right, sir?" Brian asked, hurrying over to see if the store owner was hurt.

"It's just a bruise, I'm sure, but it'll be worth it to get this young hoodlum in jail," Mr. Lytell said as he mopped his forehead with his handkerchief.

"I don't know what he's talking about," the young man cried. "My name's Stu Compton, and I never robbed anybody! I came in here five minutes ago to buy some bread, and this old man jumped me. Of course I fought back! Wouldn't you? But I didn't rob him. Why, I wasn't even in the United States last month. I spent all of July hiking around England."

Mr. Lytell looked stubborn. "You robbed my store on July the fourth," he snapped. "My store was the only one open that day. I took in a lot of money, and you stole it!"

"You're wrong, Pops," Stu Compton sneered. "On the Fourth of July, I was watching the best fireworks display I've ever seen—over Buckingham Palace! You've made a mistake!"

"I don't know if you robbed the store," Trixie told the young man, "but I do know that you're lying now. You weren't in London that day. You're the one who made the mistake."

What mistake did Stu Compton make?

AT THE BALL

1. **WHAT A SUPER CHARITY BALL, DI!**

   IT REALLY IS, BUT I'M GLAD TO SEE SERGEANT MOLINSON HERE, EVEN IF HE'S NOT IN UNIFORM.

2. **WHY, TRIXIE? THESE PEOPLE WOULDN'T ROB US.**

   LOOK AT MRS. BOYER'S JEWELS. SERGEANT MOLINSON SAID THAT JENNY THE JEWEL THIEF MIGHT BE IN THIS PART OF THE STATE.

3. **WHAT HAPPENED TO THE LIGHTS?**

4. **MY JEWELS ARE GONE!**

HOW DID
JENNY
GIVE
HERSELF
AWAY?

LEGENDS AND FOLKLORE

"I made up a couple cliff-hanger quizzes about legends and such for you," Brian told his friends. "All you have to do is guess the ending. It won't be easy, though."

1. GRETCHEN AND THE WHITE MUSTANG

Though the beautiful white mustang lived many, many years, four-year-old Gretchen was the only person ever known who had actually touched it.

Gretchen's family were pioneers traveling to Texas. The little girl was happiest when her parents tied her (so she wouldn't fall) on an old, blind mare that carried sacks of cornmeal behind the wagon.

While a wagon wheel was being fixed, the old mare wandered toward a river. Across it was the white mustang. When he whinnied, the mare plunged through the river and followed him to his wild herd.

The herd smelled the cornmeal on the mare's back and tried to get it, hurting Gretchen in their zeal. The white mustang fought them away, bit through the ropes holding the little girl, then picked her up by her dress and set her on the ground, where she fell asleep.

When Gretchen woke up the next morning,

a. the white stallion led her to a cave where an old Indian woman lived. Until the old woman died nine years later, she raised Gretchen in the ways of her tribe.

b. she saw a handsome Indian chief and many braves and squaws making food and clothes. Suddenly, they turned into the white mustang and his wild herd. One night each week, they took the form of humans and prepared the things Gretchen needed until she was old enough to care for herself.

c. the white mustang picked her up and put her on the old, blind mare's back, then disappeared. The old mare found the way back to the pioneers' camp with Gretchen still safe on her back.

d. she held on to the tail of the white mustang, and it led her back to her parents. The beautiful stallion galloped off just in time to escape being captured by others in the camp.

2. SPUYTEN DUYVIL (SPITE THE DEVIL)

It was dark that fateful Saturday night, and it was a long row back over Tappan Zee to the hamlet of Spuyten Duyvil, where Rambout Van Dam lived. He had been reveling with friends until after midnight, and now he was about to embark for home.

"Don't go! Don't go!" his friends pleaded. "Stay the night here if you wish to avoid—"

"Hah!" scoffed Van Dam. "I know that curse: 'Woe to him who travels on the Sabbath, for his way will be the way of the Devil!' Hah! I've not met the Devil yet, and I don't aim to now."

Those were the last words his friends ever heard him speak—because

a. he met the Devil and was struck dumb.

b. neither he nor his boat were seen again. (But between midnight and dawn on many Sabbath days, his oars can still be heard as he tries vainly to reach Spuyten Duyvil.)

c. he took advantage of the belief in the curse and ran off with a fortune in gold he had stolen little by little from his friends.

d. he was doomed to row the Zee forever, listening to an endless sermon by a preacher seated in the stern.

95

POPPYCOCK AND PUFFINS

"Here's a quiz," Mart said, "that might look like stuff and nonsense, but it isn't. . . . On second thought, I guess some of it is about stuff, and some is about nonsense!"

1. If someone said, "That's a lot of POPPYCOCK," would you expect to
   a. eat it?   b. admire it?   c. ignore it?

2. If someone remarked about the WHITE ELEPHANT in your attic, what might be your most fitting answer?
   a. "Buying hay for it keeps me poor."
   b. "No doubt there are quite a few more up there."
   c. "Do you like the ghost next to it, too?"

3. If someone offered you his GOOBERS, would you
   a. say, "Thanks; now my feet won't get wet"?
   b. take as many as you think you should?
   c. say, "No, thanks; I have a treeful of them myself"?

4. And how about BLOOPERS? Would you be likely to
   a. order a dozen?
   b. say, "Not for me! I never wear them"?
   c. take great pains to avoid them?

5. If you bought a SNOOD, would you be likely to
   a. use it for draining vegetables?
   b. hang your hair in it?
   c. put a leash on it and take it for a walk?

6. If you just happened to spot a PUFFIN, would you be most likely to
   a. send it to the cleaners?
   b. put it on your head?
   c. watch it quietly?

JEWEL THIEF!

Sergeant Molinson, Sleepyside's top police officer, asked Trixie to help him spot a jewel thief in a crowded department store. The thief is wearing a white dress with black polka dots and a black collar and a small black hat with a white feather.

Trixie spotted her in less than a minute. Can you?

MISER MOONEY'S MONEY

Trixie hurried to the clubhouse, where Jim had called an emergency meeting of the Bob-Whites.

"I need your help," Jim announced. "A friend of mine, Jeff Potter, has been arrested for stealing. He says he's innocent, and I believe him. The thing is, someone else must be guilty. But who?"

"Tell us about it," Honey said.

"It happened last week," Jim began. "Miser Mooney was robbed of all his money, which he kept in a cash box under his bed. Only four people could have taken it: Lillian Banks, his housekeeper; Robert Linley, Jr., his nephew; Mabel Richards, the maid; and Jeff, the gardener. The money is still missing."

"Did the thief leave any clues?" Mart asked.

"The thief didn't," Jim answered, "but Miser Mooney did. He must have seen who took his money as he lay ill in bed. He died that same night, but the police found a message on the bedside table."

"What kind of message, Jim?" Trixie asked.

"Miser Mooney had no pencil or paper," Jim explained, "but he did have a box full of drinking straws. He'd arranged them to form these three numbers."

Jim drew this picture of the straws on a piece of paper for his friends.

Brian sighed. "Seven one seven. Or maybe it's seven, exclamation mark, seven. It doesn't make much sense to me."

"It didn't make much sense to Sergeant Molinson, either," Jim told them, "until he remembered that Jeff had taken the day off to visit his mother. He'd traveled back to Miser Mooney's house on the seven-seventeen commuter train from New York City."

"Seven one seven," Dan muttered. "Seven seventeen. Yes, it fits. Too bad, Jim. It looks like your friend is guilty."

"No," Trixie said slowly, "the guilty person is—"

Who is the guilty person?

SURPRISE GIFT

Honey bought something new for Trixie's horse as a surprise gift. But Trixie had to unscramble the pictures below before Honey would give her the gift.

If you discover what the girl in the pictures below did first, and then put the pictures in order according to what she did next, the letters in the upper left corners of the pictures will spell out the name of the surprise gift.

HINT: The first picture is **not** number 1 or number 6.

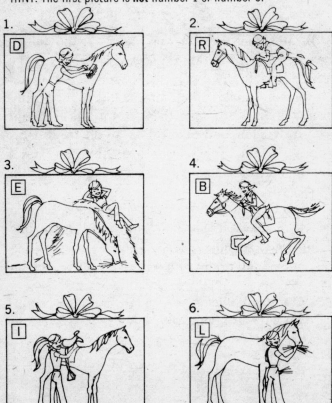

FOWL PLAY

Trixie is on a bird hunt. To test his sister's sleuthing powers, Brian Belden has hidden the name of a bird in each sentence below. Trixie spotted each name as easily as a pelican spots fish. See if you can match Trixie's fowl findings.

Sample: They moved here from Caldwell, <u>Ark</u>ansas.

1. The decrepit mansion shuddered and groaned in the howling winter wind.

2. On the tray stood a silver service for tea, gleaming in the morning sunlight.

3. The tiny tot executed a very fast, though awkward, dance.

4. The drum's throb in the dense jungle matched the throb of the frightened explorer's heart.

5. Please list the words *asp*, *arrow*, *adamant*, and *anthropology* in alphabetical order.

6. The magician placed the card in a little leather bag and handed it to her assistant.

7. A mechanic in greasy overalls stood holding a monkey wrench in one hand and a tire chain in the other.

8. Because the antique shop contains so much valuable bric-a-brac, rowdy children are not allowed in the store.

9. The social studies teacher was suspicious enough to scan A. R. Young's and M. E. Bryant's term papers for similarities.

10. A gullible person will, of course, believe outrageous things that other people tell him.

THE ACCIDENT

Mr. Johnson was conducting the London Philharmonic Orchestra in his living room as Trixie Belden and Di Lynch rang his doorbell. Not that the London Philharmonic Orchestra was actually in Mr. Johnson's house on Third Street, of course, but there was an excellent recording on his stereo of the orchestra performing a Mozart sonata, and Mr. Johnson enjoyed conducting.

"Leading a recorded orchestra is quite satisfying," the old man said when he opened the door. "The first violinist never dozes off and forgets his cue. Now, you sit down until the performance is over. Then I'll give you my donation for the Sleepyside Community Fund."

The girls sat on a stiff, prickly old sofa, watching Mr. Johnson conduct and listening to the soft, clear, precise notes of the sonata.

Suddenly, they heard pounding footsteps, and the doorbell rang a loud, frantic ring.

"Oh, phoo!" Mr. Johnson exclaimed. He put

his baton down on the music stand and went to answer the door.

A rumpled, wild-eyed man stood on the doorstep. His necktie was askew, and he had a handkerchief wrapped around one hand.

"I need help!" he said. His voice was very hoarse. "An accident. We hit a tree, right up the street. My wife . . . in the car! Can you come?"

"Good heavens!" Mr. Johnson swung the door wide. "Trixie! Di! Call the police! Call an ambulance! I'll go with this gentleman and. . . ."

Trixie already had the telephone receiver to her ear. "Hello," she said, "Sleepyside Police Department? I'm calling from fourteen twenty-seven Third Street, and there's a man here who's faking a car accident. Can you send someone . . . ?"

Trixie got no further before the stranger in the doorway glared at her, then fled into the night.

"My word!" exclaimed Mr. Johnson. "How very remarkable. He—he seems to be quite all right."

"He sure does," declared Trixie, "because there was no accident!"

How did Trixie know this?

THE INJURED NEIGHBOR

1. MOMS SAID TO KNOCK FIRST, THEN GO ON IN. SINCE MRS. STOKES FELL YESTERDAY, SHE CAN'T GET OUT OF BED.

2. WE THOUGHT YOU MIGHT LIKE SOME FLOWERS, MRS. STOKES. ARE YOU FEELING BETTER TODAY?

NO, I'M NOT. AND I'M GOING TO SUE THE HAKAITO BROTHERS. IT WAS THEIR WALK I TRIPPED ON.

3. WOULD YOU LIKE ME TO PUT THESE FLOWERS IN SOME WATER FOR YOU?

4. OF COURSE. THERE'S A VASE ON THE KITCHEN COUNTER.

I'LL DO IT, DI.

5. I FOUND THE VASE, AND IT'S JUST THE RIGHT SIZE.

6. WHAT A BEAUTIFUL VASE! THE FLOWERS LOOK LOVELY IN THEM.

ARE YOU REALLY GOING TO SUE THE HAKAITOS?

7. I CERTAINLY AM. I MAY NEVER WALK AGAIN. I CAN'T RELY ON NEIGHBORS TO BRING OVER ALL MY MEALS, AND HOUSEKEEPERS ARE EXPENSIVE.

8. I'M SORRY YOU'RE HURT, MRS. STOKES, BUT I KNOW THAT YOU'VE BEEN WALKING AROUND THIS VERY MORNING.

HOW DID TRIXIE KNOW THAT?

MART'S MOTHER GOOSE

When Mart sat down to read to six-year-old Bobby, he couldn't resist reciting Mother Goose in his own special way. Can you figure out which simple nursery rhymes Mart turned into convoluted complexities?

1. Maria maintained a diminutive cosset; the lanuginous integument of said mutton mammal struck all as being as niveous as neve.

2. "O stripling of the animalcular lapis lazulian appearance, tend hither and concertize on thy canorous contrivance—Yon lambkin's within the confines of the mead; yon bovine's in proximity to the maize."

3. An antiquated female at one time endured existence within the boundaries of a cothernus. The aforementioned progenitress nurtured such a multifarious amassment of pubescent bipeds that she had absolutely no cognizance of what *modus operandi* to perpetrate.

4. "Grimalkin, grimalkin, whence hast thou betaken thyself?"
   "I've promenaded through yon municipality (famed for its descending viaduct) to descry and ogle the female personage who rulest as thy acknowledged sovereign."

5. Alliterative adolescents of antonymous genders peregrinated upward on a monticule with the explicit expectation of seizing and transporting a piggin of transpicuous fluid.

WORD LADDERS

Trixie claims that solving Word Ladders will help her do better in her English class at school—in spelling, anyway. The rest of the Bob-Whites just laugh among themselves about it. They know that Trixie likes Word Ladders because they're like mysteries to be solved. You try them and decide who's right, Trixie or her friends.

Start with the word at the top (or the bottom) and change just one letter at a time for each rung of the ladder until you reach the other end. Each rung must have a real word on it. If you need more rungs than are shown, that's okay, but when you've done a few, you probably won't need any extras.

> **Sample:**
> C A T
> C O T
> D O T
> D O G

CARD	HATE	BIRD	BOOK	JAIL
____	____	____	COOK	BAIL
____	____	____	CORK	BALL
GAME	LOVE	____	PORK	BALK
		CAGE	PARK	BACK
			MARK	LACK
				LOCK

107

THE
BOARDER

"Reddy, come here!" cried Trixie Belden. She raced after the Irish setter, around the corner from Elm Street onto Parsons Court.

"That's what I like!" teased Honey Wheeler as she trotted after Trixie. "An obedient dog!"

"Reddy! Stop that!" Trixie shouted as the dog chased a squirrel across Mrs. Trevino's front lawn. The squirrel scooted up into the big elm tree at the corner of the Trevino property, and when it reached the safety of the lower branches, it stopped and began to scold the dog.

Mrs. Trevino's front door opened, and a young man came down the steps of the house and went toward the car that sat at the curb. Reddy immediately forgot the squirrel and romped over to play with the man.

"Please call off your dog." The man's voice cracked with fear as he spoke to Trixie. His car keys clinked together as they dangled from his trembling fingers.

"Reddy, behave!" Trixie ran and took the dog by his collar. "I'm sorry," she told the man. "He's a good dog, but he doesn't mind very well. Are you Mrs. Trevino's new boarder?"

"Yes." The man hurried around to the driver's seat.

"I hope you'll like it here in Sleepyside," Trixie told him. "Mrs. Trevino said you'd be coming today. We've all been excited about it. We don't get a new English teacher at the high school every day. My name's Trixie Belden."

"And I'm Honey Wheeler," said her companion.

"I'm happy to meet you girls," said the man. "If all my students are as nice as you, I won't have nothing to complain about."

He drove away then, and a moment later, Mrs. Trevino's little gray sedan turned into the street.

"Two-one-one-N-Y-S," Trixie said. "Remember that, Honey. Two-one-one-N-Y-S! That's his license number. We may need it to tell the police, because whoever that man is, he's no English teacher!"

Why was Trixie so certain that the man had lied to them?

FOOD FOR THOUGHT

"This quiz offers food for thought only," Honey told Mart, "but I think you'll like it anyway. Try to fill in all the blanks in a minute."

1. Too many _____ spoil the _____ .

2. Don't count your _____ before they're hatched.

3. A watched _____ never _____ .

4. Half a _____ is better than none.

5. Don't cry over spilled _____ .

6. One man's _____ is another man's poison.

7. Don't put all your _____ in one basket.

8. What's sauce for the _____ is sauce for the _____ .

9. An _____ a day keeps the doctor away.

10. The proof of the _____ is in the eating.

11. You can't have your _____ and eat it, too.

12. A rotten _____ spoils the whole barrel.

13. You can catch more flies with _____ than with _____ .

14. Variety is the _____ of life.

15. There's more than one _____ in the ocean.

QUICKIE QUIZ #2

Trixie's adventures are sometimes scary, but she's very glad they aren't as fantastic as those that happened to Dorothy in L. Frank Baum's **The Wonderful Wizard of Oz.**

What was the name of Dorothy's dog? What were the names of her three companions? What did each want from the Wizard?

SIGN LANGUAGE

"I can read these signs, Trixie," her little brother, Bobby, said, " 'cause there aren't any hard words on them."

In fact, there aren't any words at all! They are international road signs. Can you match each sign with its meaning?

1. Pedestrian Crossing

2. Two-way Traffic

3. Right Lane Ends

4. Slippery When Wet

5. No U-turn

6. School Crossing

7. No Right Turn

8. Divided Highway Ends

9. Merge (Ease into main traffic)

10. School zone

11. No Left Turn

12. Divided Highway

THE
COIN TOSS

It was a cold, almost blizzardy day as the Bob-Whites scurried into Wimpy's Hamburger Parlor. Inside, it was very warm. Excitement was in the air. It was time for the hamburger contest.

Many teen-agers had entered, but attention was riveted upon Mart Belden, the Bob-Whites' entry, and Bernie Judd, last year's champion. Bernie was a member of the Snow Devils, a snowmobile club that boasted the toughest members, the best snowmobiles, and the fanciest outfits. Even their goggles, which they never took off in public, were specially designed with white devil-figures on the frames.

"They give a trophy to whoever eats the most hamburgers in fifteen minutes," Trixie explained to her cousin Hallie, who was visiting from Idaho. "I'm sure Mart will win this year!"

"A veritable verity," Mart agreed, "if I get to sit on my lucky stool. That stool and my appetite will be a winning combination."

As Mart hurried to claim his favorite seat, Bernie Judd made a rush for it, too. "Back off, Belden," he snarled. "I was here first!"

"Back off yourself!" Mart snapped. "*I* was here first!"

"Listen, you two," Brian said, "that stool isn't really lucky. You guys only think it is. Why not toss a coin for it?"

Bernie, who was much huskier than Mart, was about to refuse, when he saw another Snow Devil, big Tug Johnson, enter the Parlor. "Okay," Bernie said quickly, "we'll toss for it— and I'll do the tossing!"

Bernie spun a quarter into the air. "I call heads," he said, smacking the coin onto the back of his hand. In the next second, he had stuffed the coin back into his pocket. "Heads it was," he announced. "The seat's mine!"

"Oh, no, you don't," Mart yelped. "I saw that quarter, and it came up tails!"

Tug Johnson was at Bernie's side. "You're wrong," he said, grinning. "I saw the whole thing, and I give you my word that the coin came up heads."

"There!" Bernie told the crowd with a smirk. "That proves it!"

"No, Bernie," Trixie told him. "The only thing it proves is that Tug's word is no good."

Why not?

CRYPTIC LISTS

Each of the following lists of related words is in code.
Every letter stands for another letter. Each list has its own
code. Crack the codes and decipher the cryptic words.
We've given you a "bit" of help with the first code.

A

Trixie and her friends love
to ride horses, and these
words all have something to
do with horses.

Example: saddle

  b i t
1. R Y J

  b i
2. R H Y T B U

   t i
3. I J Y H H K F

4. W Q B B E F

   i
5. H U Y D I

  t t
6. J H E J

  t b
7. I J Q R B U

8. X E H I U I X E U

B

Trixie lives just north of
New York City. Here are
some sights she might see
when she visits that city.

Example: Rockefeller Plaza.

1. M R Z J K   K G O B I J

2. N I J J A S R F P   Q R X X B N J

3. D I C B H S B W

4. J Z E R I J   K M B M J

  D O R X H R A N

5. Z B H R K C A   K G O B I J

  N B I H J A

6. F C A J W   R K X B A H

7. K M B M O J   C L   X R D J I M W

8. F J A M I B X   E B I V

114

C

Here are some of the crimes that Trixie has solved.

Example: theft

1. ZLRKQBOCBFQFKD
2. OLYYBOV
3. PJRDDIFKD
4. HFAKXMMFKD
5. XOPLK
6. COXRA
7. YRODIXOV
8. SXKAXIFPJ

D

Here are some means of transportation that Trixie and her friends have used.

Example: horse

1. VQANNI OBV
2. XTMCL
3. OCQJQIU
4. VXMXCNL FMYNL
5. ZCQGBZ XTBQG
6. QMLNU
7. MCTZIMLU
8. DML

QUICKIE QUIZ #3

*Trixie and her brothers call their mother "Moms."
By what unusual name do the girls in Louisa May
Alcott's* Little Women *call their mother? Can you
also name the four "Little Women"? What is their
last name, and what is their father's occupation?*

THE RE- PORTER'S CODE

1. DID YOU SEE THAT, TRIXIE? THAT WOMAN WAS GAGGED!

I GOT THE LICENSE PLATE NUMBER. LET'S CALL THE POLICE, QUICK!

2. GLEEPS, BRIAN, WHAT DO WE DO FIRST?

ONE OF THEM IS HURT. I'LL HELP HIM AND YOU UNTIE ONE OF THE WOMEN. THEN GET TO THAT PHONE WHILE SHE UNTIES THE OTHERS.

3. THEY KIDNAPPED DELORES, AND THEY HIT FRANK WITH A BLACKJACK.

4. I THINK HE'LL BE ALL RIGHT, BUT YOU'D BETTER CALL AN AMBULANCE, TOO, TRIXIE, JUST TO BE SAFE.

5. THE LICENSE PLATE NUMBER DIDN'T HELP, TRIXIE...THEY USED A STOLEN VEHICLE.

WHAT

DID IT

SAY?

117

STOLEN DIAMONDS

Trixie sighed as she and handsome Jim Frayne posed for one last photograph in the London airport. "I wish we could solve just one more mystery here before we go home," she said.

Brian chuckled. "See if you can solve this case I read about in this morning's newspaper. It involves a jewel thief who almost outwitted Scotland Yard's best man.

"It happened last night in a luxury apartment building. Since it was a holiday, the place was almost deserted. About nine-thirty, Scotland Yard received a frantic telephone call. Someone had broken into Lady Frobisher's apartment and robbed her of a diamond necklace worth a fortune. The Yard inspector and some of his men were nearby, working on another case. Within minutes of the crime, they had the building surrounded."

"Did Lady Frobisher give the police the thief's description?" Jim asked.

"She couldn't," Brian replied. "The thief wore a ski mask and a thick, shapeless topcoat. Sure that the thief couldn't leave the building without getting caught, the police began to search the place. They went first to apartments where there were lights on.

"The only person they found on Lady Frobisher's floor was an elderly man who said he'd been reading and didn't know anything. The inspector saw an open book and reading glasses on a small table beside an overstuffed chair.

"In an upstairs apartment was a woman wearing dark glasses. She explained that she was blind. She wasn't afraid to live alone—she had done so quite capably for several years. In spite of her acute hearing, though, she said she hadn't heard any suspicious sounds.

"The last suspect, the doorman, claimed he didn't know anything, either. But he was in his basement apartment instead of at his post when the police arrived at the scene!"

"If that's the whole story, I haven't figured out who the thief was," Jim said. Then he gazed fondly at Trixie and added, "I'm sure Trixie has, though."

Trixie blushed a little as she said, "Brian told the story very well, but I'm sure the inspector arrested the—"

Whom *did* the inspector arrest?

THE OBJECT OF THE MYSTERY

NOTE: This is a special quiz for readers of TRIXIE BELDEN mysteries.

The questions below are related to various Bob-White adventures. Following each question is the title of the book in the TRIXIE BELDEN series that the question relates to. Match the objects on the pages with the questions they answer. There are more objects than questions, so watch out!

1. Although he didn't know it, Spider Webster found something that helped Trixie identify the villain who was trying to steal Juliana's inheritance. What was it? **The Mystery of the Missing Heiress**

2. What did Mart borrow from a friend that helped prove Di's "Uncle Monty" was an impostor? **The Mysterious Visitor**

3. What were the Bob-Whites searching for when Trixie almost drowned in a sinkhole during a sudden downpour? **The Mystery at Bob-White Cave**

4. Where did Trixie find the cryptic map that led to the capture of South American revolutionaries who were stockpiling stolen guns? **Mystery on the Mississippi**

5. What was Trixie's only clue to the identity of the sinister figure who tried to crush the Bob-Whites under a falling tree? **Mystery at Mead's Mountain**

6. What did Trixie, Honey, and Jim have with them during their long night's vigil atop a barn as floodwaters crept higher and higher? **The Happy Valley Mystery**

7. Where did Trixie find the enigmatic verse that put the Bob-Whites and their Iowa friends on the trail of three ruthless international jewel thieves? **The Mystery of the Blinking Eye**

8. Bobby fell and cut his knee on something in an old abandoned cottage—something that eventually brought Trixie face-to-face with a cunning pickpocket. What was it? **The Gatehouse Mystery**

9. When Trixie and Honey found the mysterious "poacher" they'd been tracking in the Wheeler game preserve, he returned something Trixie had lost when her horse was spooked by gunshots. What was it? **The Mystery Off Glen Road**

10. What did Mart and Trixie use to attract the attention of Spider Webster when they were being held captive in the Lynches' trailer? **The Mysterious Visitor**

11. While investigating the theft of Hoppy from the roof of Town Hall, what did Trixie find, stuck under a shingle, that placed her prime suspect at the scene of the crime? **The Mystery of the Phantom Grasshopper**

12. The theft of this object from the Bob-White station wagon created a loose end that Trixie couldn't tie up with her theory in the case of the missing Ming vase. What was the stolen object? **The Mystery of the Headless Horseman**

13. What did Trixie find in the Wheelers' attic that later made it possible for her to send Jim a silent call for help? **The Mysterious Code**

14. What did a pack rat leave on the roof of Hallie Belden's tent that provided a clue to the mystery encountered by the B.W.G.'s in a northern Idaho wilderness camp? **The Sasquatch Mystery**

15. While working on a fund-raising project for the school art department, what did Trixie find that provided her first clue to the gang of criminals operating out of an abandoned house? **The Mystery Off Old Telegraph Road**

ANSWERS

Page 9, FINGERPRINTS

1.true 2.false (They also appear on palms and on soles of feet.) 3.true (There are eight basic patterns.) 4.false 5.false 6.true 7.false 8.true 9.true 10.false (At least one criminal had smooth skin grafted to his fingertips. An officer, talking to him about hitchhiking, became suspicious at the sight of the extremely smooth skin on the hitchhiker's fingertips. The suspicion led to an investigation, and the man's criminal background was uncovered—all because he had no prints!).

Page 10, MYSTERY AT WIMPY'S

Trixie had a hamburger and a vanilla shake; Jim and Honey had hamburgers and chocolate shakes; Mart and Brian had cheeseburgers and vanilla shakes.

Page 10, THE CASE OF THE TRICKY TATTOOS

Jailbird Joe.

Page 11, THE CASE OF THE AMATEUR BURGLAR

In failing to open the safe with his tools, the burglar also failed to notice the combination to the safe on the desk, and he left behind his crowbar! He rifled the wallet on the desk, but didn't see the hundred-dollar bill in the pencil holder or the car keys in the drawer. He left his footprint on the floor (along with his glove), and in his haste to escape, he left a piece of his jacket snagged on a nail!

Pages 12–13, THE GUEST

Any true Romanian would know that Count Dracula was a real person who lived in the Carpathians centuries ago, and that he was not simply a character in a book and a motion picture. Mrs. Wheeler called the Bronsons and learned that they had never even met a Mr. Ivanescu. She then called the police, who identified him as a confidence man from New Jersey. He read the society pages of newspapers to get information about wealthy people who might invest money in phony schemes.

Pages 14–15, MUSEUM MYSTERY

Trixie told the museum official to look in the stuffed penguin in the North Pole exhibit (see panel #1). She knew that penguins are native to areas around the South Pole only, and she correctly guessed that one of the workmen setting up the North Pole exhibit had stashed the missing idol in the penguin, planning to take it with him when he left.

Page 16, A QUETZAL IN A WILLIWAW?

1.b 2.a 3.c 4.b 5.a 6.b 7.c 8.a 9.c 10.a.

Page 17, SPORTS VARIETY

1.k 2.o 3.h 4.a 5.i 6.n 7.m 8.d 9.j 10.b 11.g 12.e 13.l 14.c 15.f.

Page 17, QUICKIE QUIZ #1

The dwarves' names are Happy, Sleepy, Dopey, Doc,

Bashful, Sneezy, and Grumpy. The prince was not named. (Prince Charming was the prince who married Cinderella!).

Pages 18–19, A DRINK OF COOL WATER

It was Memorial Day—a national holiday—and no mail is delivered on national holidays. Mrs. Elliot and Trixie managed to delay the man in the postal uniform until the police arrived. The bogus mail carrier had a bag stuffed with Mrs. Elliot's silverware. He had used a fake post office uniform to get into several houses in the area, then asked for water. He picked up anything that looked valuable when his unsuspecting victims went to the kitchen to get him a drink.

Page 20, THE CHALLENGE

By placing one log across the curve, and the second log from the midpoint of the first one to the opposite bank, Brian was able to cross the stream without getting wet.

Page 20, R U 4 K9's, 2?

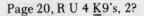

Mart: Are you busy? Trixie: Why, yes. Why? Mart: I am uneasy. Trixie: Why are you uneasy? Mart: I see a

127

seedy canine. Trixie: *You* can see a tepee in a tenement! Mart: I wonder if anyone else sees him. Trixie: I see him, too. He isn't seedy—he's a cutie! Mart: Oh, you are an ally of all canines. His behavior is deviate. Trixie: Anyone can see he's benign. Mart: Okay, okay. I can see he's a benign canine, too. Excuse me!

Page 21, SPELUNKING

1.false 2.true (Grains of sand are covered with layers of limewater that harden.) 3.true 4.true 5.Millicent was enjoying a cool breeze that came from deep underground through a crack in the rocks that made up part of the cave ceiling.

Pages 22–23, THE SLEEPING PILOT

The pilot lied when he said he didn't wake up till his alarm went off "this morning." His alarm was set for ten o'clock (see panel #7)—just an hour after he claimed he went to bed!

Pages 24–25, SNEAK THIEF

If the thief had broken the window from the outside, the glass would have fallen into the library rather than onto the porch. Also, the geese would have made a commotion. (Geese are famous for being both noisy and vicious "watchdogs.") When the police questioned the new housekeeper, she confessed.

Page 26, ABOUT THIS AND THAT

1.false (A gallon of milk weighs eight pounds; a

gallon of gas weighs six pounds.) 2.true (The rest is shell.) 3.false (His name was Angel.) 4.true 5.false (It has twelve letters.) 6.true (Water goes down the drain clockwise in the northern hemisphere, counterclockwise in the southern hemisphere.) 7.true (Easter falls between March 22 and April 25.) 8.true 9.false (Banana oil is not made of bananas; it just smells like bananas.) 10.false.

Pages 27–28, MR. LYTELL'S GENERAL STORE

1.yes 2.no 3.yes 4.yes 5.yes 6.yes 7.yes 8.yes 9.yes 10.no 11.no 12.yes 13.no 14.yes 15.no 16.no 17.yes 18.yes 19.yes 20.yes.

Page 29, BAFFLERS

1.a rainbow 2.a traffic light 3.a stamp.

Pages 30–31, SLEEPYSIDE BANK MYSTERY

Trixie told her father that Ms. Clarendon was probably a phony, because a stamp collector is a *philatelist*. A *philologist* is a person who studies language.

Pages 32–33, FAMOUS FICTIONAL DETECTIVES

1.Sam Spade 2.Sherlock Holmes 3.Jane Marple 4.Tubby Tompkins in *Little Lulu*® 5.Father Brown 6.Jim Rockford 7.Lieutenant Columbo 8.The Hardy Boys 9.Inspector Closseau 10.Nancy Drew 11.The Shadow 12.Charlie Chan 13.Perry Mason 14.Leroy "Encyclopedia" Brown 15.Charlie's Angels.

Pages 34–35, THE COMPANION

Trixie simply took Mrs. Garber to the door. The snow had stopped falling the night before, yet there were no tracks made by any kind of vehicle—only those made by Trixie and Bobby were there (see panel #1). Even with her limited vision, Mrs. Garber could see that. Bella was dismissed immediately.

Pages 36–37, A FAMOUS PAINTING

Honey knew that George and Martha Washington never moved into the White House. The executive mansion was not completed until 1800, by which time John Adams was President.

Page 38, HORSE THIEVES!

Realizing at once that the handwritten numbers referred to the words on the same line, Trixie read the message—"Bring trailer after second (event). Lady's guard out of way." The police apprehended the thieves as they were leading Lady into their trailer.

Page 39, MISSING PARTNERS

1.wear 2.socks 3.cents 4.butter 5.Clark 6.eye 7.shoulders 8.key 9.span 10.dance 11.thread 12.bat 13.day 14.ends 15.nails 16.Wendy 17.white 18.fork 19.Remus 20.forth 21.ladder 22.coat 23.outs 24.dagger 25.the beast 26.pains 27.saddle 28.shut 29.Goliath 30.sevens 31.bows 32.lace 33.flats 34.Esau 35.silver 36.ink 37.rain 38.pans 39.pepper 40.Eve.

Page 40-41, PIRATES BOLD

1.He buried some of it on Long Island in full view of witnesses who could inform authorities (or dig it up for themselves). 2.aboard ship 3.black, skull and crossbones, skeleton (or cutlasses) 4.a (cooked slowly on wooden grills called *boucans*) 5.all of these 6.a (a dish of several kinds of foods) 7.no (The crew owned it with the captain.) 8.old Spanish money worth about one dollar 9.yes 10.a–Blackbeard b–Jean Lafitte c–Henry Morgan d–Captain Kidd.

Pages 42-43, GRIMM CASTLE

Jim said he was driving an English car. But passengers there sit to the left of the driver, who is on the right, just opposite of drivers in most parts of the world. Thus Jim would only have been able to see the right side of the ghost's face, once the specter became a passenger in the English automobile, and not the left side with the wart.

Pages 44-45, STATE NAMES AND NICKNAMES

1.Missouri 2.California 3.Georgia 4.Alaska 5.Florida 6.Michigan 7.Louisiana 8.Vermont 9.Arizona 10.Iowa 11.Indiana 12.Rhode Island 13.Oklahoma 14.Utah 15.Delaware.

Page 45, STUMPERS

1.one (You can ride the very same horse every day.) 2.Both were right. The great-grandfather was teasing a little, though. In the room were the great-grandfather, his son, his grandson, and his great-granddaughter. Considering all the relationships, the great-grandfather was correct: He, his son, and his grandson were all fathers. He and his son each had a grandchild, and so on.

Pages 46–47, THE SAFE ROBBER

The nephew said the thief ran out the kitchen door, yet the large spider web in the doorway (see panel #4) was undisturbed. The nephew had tried to steal his uncle's money and collect theft insurance, too! Thanks to Trixie, he didn't get away with it.

Pages 48–49, THE MISSING WILL

The peacock would hardly be defending *her* nest. A pea*cock* is a male bird—and a pea*hen* is the female of the species—as wildlife expert Ned Smith would have known. Mr. Hartman found the missing will tucked behind "Polly's" photograph.

Pages 50–51, DOODLERS' NOODLERS

1.free throw 2.figure skating 3.hole in one 4.heavyweight crown 5.turkey 6.fourth down 7.shortstop 8.flying rings 9.steeplechase 10.match point 11.triple crown 12.quarterback.

Pages 52–53, LIZARDS AND LUCK

1.Your teeth may fall out. 2.It's good luck, so they say, to try on the right shoe first. 3.Say "One leaf for fame; one leaf for wealth; one leaf for honor; one leaf for health." 4.Under your bed. 5.You must not tell it. 6.Say "What do you want?" 7.Put something like a broom or a piece of mesh at the entrance, and the witch will have to stop to count the broom bristles or mesh holes, which will probably take her until daylight, when she must disappear. 8.Own it. 9.Turn the beetle right side up. 10.Close the books—so what you learned won't fall out. (With any luck, it won't fall out of your head, either!).

Page 53, ONCE IS TOO MUCH

Every ingredient in the recipe is poisonous!

Page 80, COUNT-ATHON

Ms. Dupuis paid Trixie $7.90.

Page 81, IT'S TRUE . . . IT'S FALSE . . . OH, I GIVE UP!

1.no 2.no 3.no 4.no (not Illinois but Kentucky) 5.no 6.yes 7.yes (not *Sputnik* but the moon!) 8.no 9.no 10.yes (not Ireland but Scotland).

Pages 82–83, TROUBLE IN THE DESERT

The man in the cabin said he lived there alone. Trixie saw hair oil and a hairbrush on the dresser (see panel #5)—but the man was quite bald! When the police checked the cabin, they found its real occupant tied up in a storage room. The bald man was, of course, the armed robber the Bob-Whites had heard about on Mart's radio.

Pages 84–85, THE DISAPPEARING DIAMONDS

Trixie figured that the thief slipped the rings into an envelope, then stepped into the post office next door and mailed the diamonds to himself. Trixie's hunch was right; the next day the police stepped in the moment the thief opened his mail—and they found the diamonds!

Pages 86–87, HORSES AND HORSE RACING

1.c 2.a 3.c 4.d 5.b 6.d 7.c 8.c 9.a 10.a 11.c 12.d 13.b 14.b 15.b.

Page 88, THE MYSTERIOUS VALENTINE

Beginning with the M and reading every other letter, going completely around the heart twice, the message reads: "Meet me at the stable for a valentine horseback ride." The arrow on the map points to the Wheeler stable. The valentine is from Jim Frayne, of course.

Page 89, THE CASE OF
THE BAFFLING BANK BANDIT

Mean Mike Madison.

Page 89, THE MYSTERY OF
THE GRITTY GRADES

Di had C's in all three subjects; Honey had an A in English, a C in algebra, and a B in social studies; Trixie had B's in social studies and algebra and a C in English.

Pages 90–91, MR. LYTELL NABS A THIEF

England would hardly celebrate the United States' Independence Day! When confronted with this fact, Stu Compton broke down and confessed.

Pages 92–93, AT THE BALL

Actually, Honey spotted Jenny and didn't know it! Jenny had made herself a matching band outfit so that she could slip in as an extra player in the all-male combo, but she had made a mistake: She made the jacket with the buttons on the left side (see panels #1 and #5), as is normal for women's clothes. A man's buttons are always on the right. Honey had noticed it earlier in the evening and mentioned it to Trixie. Trixie remembered this and put two and two together in time for Sergeant Molinson to stop Jenny's escape.

Pages 94–95, LEGENDS AND FOLKLORE

1.c 2.b.

Page 96, POPPYCOCK AND PUFFINS

1.c (nonsense) 2.b (an object not valued by its owner, but which might be valued by others) 3.b (peanuts) 4.c (blunders) 5.b (net to hold the hair at the back of your head) 6.c (seabird).

Page 97, JEWEL THIEF!

The thief is the sixth woman from the left.

Pages 98–99, MISER MOONEY'S MONEY

Miser Mooney had a full box of straws, yet he'd used a torn one. Why? To dot the *i* of the middle *letter!* Read the other way up, the message spelled the name of the thief: Lillian (Lil) Banks, the housekeeper.

Page 100, SURPRISE GIFT

BRIDLE.

Page 101, FOWL PLAY

1. <u>howl</u>ing
2. <u>tea, gleam</u>ing
3. <u>though awk</u>ward
4. th<u>rob in</u>
5. *<u>asp, arrow</u>*
6. <u>card in a l</u>ittle
7. <u>wren</u>ch
8. bric-a-<u>brac, rowdy</u>
9. s<u>can A. R. Young</u>'s
10. <u>gull</u>ible

Page 102–103, THE ACCIDENT

Trixie, Di, and Mr. Johnson were listening quietly to the soft music of the Mozart sonata. Had a car hit a tree anywhere nearby, they would surely have heard the crash. They did not, so Trixie assumed, correctly, that there had been no crash. Later that evening, Mr. Johnson identified the stranger's photograph in a police mug book. The man was a grifter who lured his victims away from their homes with false accident reports. In the excitement, the victims often left their doors open, and an accomplice slipped into the houses to take any valuables left lying around. The con men would then drive away before the police were even called.

Pages 104–105, THE INJURED NEIGHBOR

There was a cake baking in the oven (see panel #5). Anyone who brought a cake to her would bring one that was already baked. Mrs. Stokes must have mixed this one herself, and she would have had to walk to the kitchen to do it.

Page 106, MART'S MOTHER GOOSE

1. "Mary Had a Little Lamb" 2. "Little Boy Blue" 3. "There Was an Old Woman Who Lived in a Shoe" 4. "Pussycat, Pussycat" 5. "Jack and Jill."

Page 107, WORD LADDERS

(Note: Other answers are possible)

CARD	HATE	BIRD	BOOK	JAIL
CARE	HAVE	BARD	COOK	BAIL
CAME	LAVE	BARE	CORK	BALL
GAME	LOVE	CARE	PORK	BALK
		CAGE	PARK	BACK
			MARK	LACK
				LOCK

Pages 108–109, THE BOARDER

An English teacher would *never*, *never* use a double negative in this ungrammatical way. The instant the man said, "I *won't* have *nothing* to complain about," Trixie was suspicious.

Mrs. Trevino had gone out without locking her

front door, and the man, who was really taking a survey for a soap company, had found the door open. He hadn't been able to resist walking in and helping himself to a pocketful of Mrs. Trevino's jewelry. He had then pretended to be her boarder when Trixie and Honey spoke to him. The police picked him up in Sleepyside's business district, and Mrs. Trevino's things were recovered.

Page 110, FOOD FOR THOUGHT

1.cooks, broth 2.chickens 3.pot, boils 4.loaf 5.milk 6.meat 7.eggs 8.goose, gander 9.apple 10.pudding 11.cake 12.apple 13.honey, vinegar 14.spice 15.fish.

Page 110, QUICKIE QUIZ #2

Toto was Dorothy's dog. Scarecrow wanted a brain, Tin Woodman wanted a heart, and Cowardly Lion wanted courage. (Dorothy wanted to go back home to Kansas.).

Page 111, SIGN LANGUAGE

1.j 2.l 3.c 4.i 5.k 6.b 7.h 8.e 9.d 10.a 11.g 12.f.

Pages 112–113, THE COIN TOSS

Tug could not have seen anything. His cold snow goggles would have fogged up as soon as he entered the warm room. Bernie finally admitted that Mart had won the toss, but the lucky stool didn't help Mart after all—a skinny kid named Merton Chun won the trophy!

A	B
1.bit	1.Times Square
2.bridle	2.Greenwich Village
3.stirrup	3.Broadway
4.gallop	4.Empire State Building
5.reins	5.Madison Square Garden
6.trot	6.Coney Island
7.stable	7.Statue of Liberty
8.horseshoe	8.Central Park

C	D
1.counterfeiting	1.school bus
2.robbery	2.train
3.smuggling	3.bicycle
4.kidnapping	4.station wagon
5.arson	5.pickup truck
6.fraud	6.canoe
7.burglary	7.airplane
8.vandalism	8.van

Page 115, QUICKIE QUIZ #3

Margaret (Meg), Josephine (Jo), Beth, and Amy
March were the four "Little Women." They called
their mother "Marmee." Their father was a chaplain
in the army.

Pages 116–117, THE REPORTER'S CODE

The reporter saw the criminals coming and guessed
where they'd take her. In her hurry to get the address
down, her fingers moved one key to the right on her

typewriter (see panel #8). Trixie realized this and gave Sergeant Molinson the correct address: 34 Hawthorne Street.

Pages 118–119, STOLEN DIAMONDS

The inspector arrested the woman, as Trixie correctly guessed. In an attempt to hide from the police, the woman had broken into the other apartment, turned the lights on, and pretended to be the tenant. She'd forgotten, however, that people who can't see don't need the lights on. She later confessed to this burglary and to several others.

Pages 120–121, THE OBJECT OF THE MYSTERY

1.f 2.k 3.q 4.t 5.c 6.r 7.g 8.s 9.a 10.m 11.o 12.h 13.e 14.l 15.b.